DANGER ON DOLPHIN ISLAND

Another You Say Which Way Adventure
by:

BLAIR POLLY

ISBN-13: 978-1518799600
ISBN-10: 1518799604

How This Book Works

- This story depends on YOU.

- YOU say which way the story goes.

- What will YOU do?

At the end of each chapter, you get to make a decision. Turn to the page that matches your choice. **P62** means turn to page 62.

There are many paths to try. You can read them all over time. Right now, it's time to start the story. Good luck.

Oh … and watch out for poachers!

Danger on Dolphin Island

Lagoon Landing

From the float plane's window, you can see how Dolphin Island got its name.

The island's shape looks like a dolphin leaping out of the water. A sparkling lagoon forms the curve of the dolphin's belly, two headlands to the east form its tail and to the west another headland forms the dolphin's nose. As the plane banks around, losing altitude in preparation for its lagoon landing, the island's volcanic cone resembles a dorsal fin on the dolphins back.

Soon every camera and cell phone is trained on the fiery mountain.

"Wow look at that volcano," shouts a kid in the seat in front of you. "There's steam coming from the crater."

The plane's pontoons kick up a rooster-tail of spray as they touch down on the lagoon's clear water. As the plane slows, the pilot revs the engine and motors towards a wooden wharf where a group of smiling locals await your arrival.

"Welcome to Dolphin Island," they say as they secure the plane, unload your bags, and assist you across the narrow gap to the safety of a small timber wharf.

Coconut palms fringe the lagoon's white-sand beach.

Palm-thatched huts poke out of the surrounding jungle. The resort's main building is just beyond the beach opposite the wharf.

Between the wharf's rustic planks you can see brightly colored fish dart back and forth amongst the coral. You stop and gaze down at the world beneath your feet.

You hear a soft squeak behind you and step aside as a young man in cut-off shorts trundles past pushing a trolley with luggage on it. He whistles a song as he passes, heading towards the main resort building. You and your family follow.

"Welcome to Dolphin Island Resort," a young woman with a bright smile and a pink flower tucked behind her ear says from behind the counter as you enter the lobby. "Here is the key to your quarters. Enjoy your stay."

Once your family is settled into their beachfront bungalow, you're eager to explore the island. You pack a flashlight, compass, water bottle, pocket knife, matches, mask, snorkel and flippers as well as energy bars and binoculars in your daypack and head out the door.

Once you hit the sand, you sit down and open the guidebook you bought before coming on vacation. Which way should you go first? You're still a little tired from the early morning flight, but you're also keen to get exploring.

As you study the map, you hear a couple of kids coming towards you down the beach.

"Hi, I'm Adam," a blond haired boy says as he draws

near.

"And I'm Jane."

The boy and girl are about your age and dressed in swimming shorts and brightly colored t-shirts, red for him and yellow for her. They look like twins. The only difference is that the girl's hair is tied in a long ponytail while the boy's hair is cropped short. Both are brown and have peeling noses. By their suntans you suspect they've been at the resort a few days already.

"What are you reading?" Adam asks.

"It's a guide book. It tells all about the wildlife and the volcano. It also says there might be pirate treasure hidden here somewhere. I'm just trying to figure out where to look first."

Jane clasps her hands in front of her chest and does a little hop. "Pirate treasure, really?"

Adam looks a little more skeptical, his brow creases as he squints down at you. "You sure they just don't say that to get the tourists to come here?"

"No, I've read up on it. They reckon a pirate ship named the *Port-au-Prince* went down around here in the early 1800s. I thought I might go exploring and see what I can find."

"Oh can we help?" Jane says. "There aren't many kids our age staying at the moment and lying by the pool all day gets a bit boring."

"Yeah," Adam agrees. "I'm sure we could be of some help if you tell us what to do. I've got a video camera on my new phone. I could do some filming."

There is safety in numbers when exploring, and three sets of eyes are better than one. But if you do find treasure, do you want to share it with two other people?

It is time to make your first decision. Do you:

Agree to take Adam and Jane along? **P5**

Or

Say no and go hunting for treasure on your own? **P9**

You have agreed to take Adam and Jane along.

You have a good feeling about the friendly twins. "Sure why not," you say. "It will be nice to have some company."

"Arrr me hearties," Jane cries out, getting into the spirit. "So where do we go first to find these pieces of eight?"

Adam glances at his sister and shakes his head. "Don't mind her. She does amateur dramatics at school. She always acts like this."

Jane frowns at her brother, closes one eye and growls out of the side of her mouth."You'd better watch it you lily-livered land lubber or I'll shave yer belly with a rusty razor then make you walk the plank!"

You can't help chuckling at Jane's pirate imitation. Even Adam cracks a smile.

Pleased to have made friends so quickly, you point to the map of the island in the guide book. "I've read that cyclones — that's what they call hurricanes in this part of the South Pacific — usually sweep down from the north. So I'm thinking we should start on the northern part of the island. I reckon that's the most likely place for a ship to hit."

Adam nods. "As good a theory as any."

"North is on the rocky side of the island," Jane says. "I know because I was talking about stars to one of the staff the other night. They showed me how to tell which way is south by using the Southern Cross." Jane points to the sky out over the reef that protects the lagoon from the ocean swells. "South is that way, so north is the opposite."

You pull out your compass. "Yep, you're dead right. I guess it's time for us to trek to the other side of the island."

"Better get some gear then," Adam says. "We'll meet you by the pool in five minutes."

While Adam and Jane go to get their stuff, you wander through reception and to the paved courtyard where your family and other tourists are sprawled on loungers around the pool.

"I'm off to the far side of the island with some friends," you tell your family. "I've packed myself some things for lunch so don't worry about me."

Your family waves you off. Their noses dive back into their books before you've taken a step.

When Jane and Adam arrive, the three of you follow a sandy path between the buildings, past more bungalows tucked in amongst the lush garden and head inland.

Before long the path narrows as it weaves its way between broad-leafed shrubs, ferns and palms. Many plants are covered in beautiful flowers of red, blue and yellow.

When you hear a loud squawk you stop and look up into the canopy. Adam and Jane look up too.

"There it is," says the sharp-eyed Jane. "See, on that branch near the top. It's got a green body, yellow wings and red head."

The parrot squawks again before swooping down and sitting on a branch not far away.

"Wow, so pretty," Jane says.

Adam pulls his cell phone and takes a few shots of the bird.

You look at Adam's phone. "Nice. I bet it's got GPS. That could come in handy if we find treasure."

"Unfortunately there's no signal on the island," Adam says, zipping the phone back into his pocket.

"That's a shame," you say. "Just as well I've got my compass then."

For about half an hour the three of you follow the main path. The ground slowly rises and the soft ferns give way to taller trees as you work your way inland around the lower slopes of the volcano.

Jane hums softly behind you.

When you come to a fork in the path you're not sure which way to go. Then Adam spots an old sign covered in vines. He pulls the greenery aside and reads the faded writing. "It says there's a waterfall ten minutes' walk to the right and a place called Smuggler's Cove straight ahead."

You pull out your guide book. "Smuggler's Cove is a small bay on the far side of the island. It's here on the map. Might be some good treasure hunting there."

"Let's go and check out the waterfall first," Jane says. "I feel like a swim."

Adam shakes his head, "I think we should go on to Smuggler's Cove and start looking for treasure."

The twins look at you. You have the deciding vote. What

should you do? It's only 10am but it's already hot and a swim would be nice. But then treasure is the main reason you've come to this side of the island.

What should you do? Do you:

Go to the waterfall and have a swim? **P16**

Or

Go on to Smuggler's Cove? **P21**

You have decided to say no and hunt for treasure on your own.

Adam and Jane look friendly enough, but you've always preferred doing things on your own.

"Thanks," you say, "but I'm a bit of a loner. I think I'll check a few things out on my own first. Maybe another time, okay?"

When their smiles disappear, you feel a little sorry for them, but you've been planning this expedition for ages and you don't want to be distracted.

"Okay," Jane says, looking down at her feet and kicking the ground. "If you change your mind let us know."

Adam shrugs and wanders a short distance down the beach where he sits in the sand and starts digging a hole with his toes. Jane joins him.

Trying to forget the look of disappointment on the twin's faces you study your guidebook. There are a couple of options you can take. The first is to head across the island to Smuggler's Cove, a sheltered inlet and only safe anchorage on the rocky, northern side of the island. The northern side, without a protective reef, is pounded constantly by ocean waves which makes it a treacherous place for ships.

The path to Smuggler's Cove runs from the resort, through the jungle, clockwise around the lower slopes of the volcano, and then winds back down to the sea. Marked on the map are a number of scenic lookout points and another path that branches off to a waterfall.

As well as maps, the guide book has numerous pictures of the native wildlife, mainly birds, insects and the various sea creatures that inhabit the lagoon. Luckily for the island's birdlife, rats and other predators like stoats, ferrets and snakes have never gained a foothold here. Nonetheless, thanks to man, a number of bird species, including three species of lorikeets are listed as endangered.

Your other option is to head along the beach to the westernmost end of the island where the rocky point protrudes out to sea. This is the point that looked like the dolphin's nose when you were in the plane and is another prime spot for ships to run aground.

A hundred yards beyond the nose-shaped point, and submerged, except at low tide, are a jagged cluster of rocks. These rocks are marked on the map as a serious hazard to navigation. The guidebook explains how three boats have fallen victim to these rocks in recent years, two of them while sailing from New Caledonia to the Cook Islands, the other a small inter-island freighter whose skipper cut the corner too sharp in an effort to outrun a fast approaching storm.

If modern sailors have had problems navigating these waters, maybe the pirates of old did too. Could this be where the *Port-au-Prince* ran aground and floundered as it tried to find shelter from the storm?

You look across the lagoon. The point is way off in the

distance where the western end of the reef meets the shore. Maybe snorkeling off the point would be the best way to find treasure.

After brief consideration, you decide to go overland to Smuggler's Cove. The day has barely begun and the temperature is already climbing. As the sun rises in the sky it will only get hotter. Walking under the jungle canopy will be much cooler. Maybe you'll even spot a lorikeet or two on the way.

Tucking your guidebook into a side pocket of your daypack, you brush the sand off your shorts and turn inland. Weaving your way through the cluster of bungalows and resort outbuildings you find a shell-covered path and enter the jungle. Within minutes you are in a different world.

Under the canopy there is a faint but constant hum of insects. Swarms of midges fly in mini-tornadoes this way and that. A bright blue butterfly flits past followed by a red-winged dragonfly. You hear lots of birdsong but so far have only seen mynas with their brown bodies, yellow eye patches and flashes of white on their wings. These bold bird are common in the South Pacific and you've seen quite a few around the resort already.

Leaves and twigs scrunch underfoot as you work your way uphill onto the lower slopes of the volcano. Flowering shrubs, vines and ferns crowd the path. Sturdy vines hang in tangles from trees.

When you see a flash of green above your head you stop

and crane your neck upward hoping to see the bird again. You suspect it's a lorikeet. Then you see it swoop down onto a bush covered in pink flowers. The bird hops along a stem and sips nectar from the flower with its long tongue. As it drinks you admire its beautiful colors. Its body is bright green. On its chest is a patch of red and there is a tuff of blue on top its head. It is a startling contrast to the more subdued colors of the birds back home.

As you watch the blue-crowned lorikeet move from flower to flower, you hear whispers and the snap of twigs on the path behind you. Turning your eyes in the direction of the sound you see a brief flash of color through the foliage, first red, then yellow. Crouching down, you ease yourself back into a large fern, pulling one of the fronds down in front of your body to act as a shield.

"Where's he gone?" Jane mumbles as she approaches your hiding spot.

"He can't be too far in front," Adam replies. "I caught a glimpse of him a few minutes ago."

You pull the fern fond down a little more and keep as still as possible. A few seconds later you hear the footsteps pass your position and head further along the path.

Once the footsteps have disappeared, you ease yourself out of the fern. Walking as quietly as possible, you take off in pursuit, keeping a sharp lookout for flashes of color ahead of you.

Should you give them a fright for following you? Maybe

you could pretend to be a dangerous animal and scare them away. You wonder if they've done much reading about the island's wildlife. Do they know that the most dangerous animal on the island is the wild pig … or is it the mosquito? You can't quite remember.

You are walking fast trying to close the gap between you and the twins when you see a flash of red in the distance you cup your hands around your mouth and growl as loud as you can. You've been to the zoo plenty of times, and you're not sure your lion impression is that realistic, but you give it your best attempt.

When you hear a frightened squeal and then see the twins rise above the surrounding shrubs as they scurry up a tree you smile.

"That seemed to work," you say to yourself.

You hide behind a tree trunk and try monkey sounds this time. "Oooh, oooh oooh!" you howl doing your best to sound like a chimpanzee. Surely they must know there aren't monkeys here on the island. "Oooh, oooh, oooh!"

The twins are still climbing. Then you see Jane stop and tilt her head. She says something to her brother then braces herself in the crook of the tree and starts scanning the area below her.

"Okay who's making monkey sounds!" she yells. "Come on, I know you're out there!"

Sprung.

You come out from behind the tree and walk along the

path. Thirty seconds later you are standing at the foot of the tree looking up at the twins.

"Why are you following me?" you ask.

Their faces are tinged with red as they start to climb down.

Jane is first to reach the ground. "Sorry. We just want some excitement."

"Yeah the resort is boring," Adam says. "Besides, we can go wherever we want. You can't stop us."

You look from one twin to the other and think. Maybe you've been a little harsh. Maybe it would be fun to have some friends to go exploring with.

"Okay. You can come along on one condition."

Suddenly the twins are smiling again.

"What's that?" Adam asks.

"I get to be expedition leader. After all I'm the one who's done the research."

The twins nod eagerly, grins spreading across their faces.

"Okay well let's get moving, we've got a bit of ground to cover before we get to Smuggler's Cove."

The three of you follow the path in single file, with you in the lead. You can hear Jane humming softly behind you.

When you come to a fork in the path you're not sure which way to go. Then Adam spots an old sign covered in vines. He pulls the greenery aside and reads the faded writing. "It says there's a waterfall off to the right. Smuggler's Cove is straight ahead."

"Let's go and check out the waterfall," Jane says. "I feel like a swim."

Adam shakes his head. "I think we should keep going and start hunting for treasure."

The twins look at you. You have the deciding vote. What should you do? It's hot and a swim would be nice. But then treasure is the reason you're here.

It is time to make a decision. Do you:

Go to the waterfall and have a swim? **P16**

Or

Go on to Smuggler's Cove? **P21**

You have decided to go to the waterfall and swim.

"I like the idea of a swim too," you say. "The treasure's been around for 150 years. I don't think it's going anywhere."

Jane picks up her pack. "I bet I can hold my breath under water longer than you!"

You like Jane. She's so enthusiastic about everything.

"Okay, well let's get going," Adam says in a grump as he moves down the path. "We'll have a quick swim and then get back to the treasure hunt okay?"

You nod and follow Adam. The path narrows and winds its way higher up the hillside. After a couple of zigzags you can see over the trees back towards the coast where waves crash white with foam on the reef. Tiny triangles of color, from the resort's fleet of sailing boats and wind surfers, dot the aqua water on the far side of the lagoon.

Before long you see a swing bridge in the distance. The swing bridge is made from woven vines. Its deck is laid with arm-thick branches chopped from the jungle. The bridge crosses a swiftly moving creek that has cut a deep channel into the side of the hillside as it races to the sea.

Adam stops when he reaches the bridge and turns around. "Do you think this is safe?"

You have a closer look. "It looks pretty sturdy so it should be safe."

About ten vines have been woven together to form the main cables. You grab hold of the bridge's handrails, also made of woven vines, and take a step.

"It feels okay," you say to the other. "Look!" You jump up and down a couple times. "It's hardly moving."

Despite your confidence, the other two wait until you've reached the far side before venturing across. Jane is first. She comes across with no problems, but when Adam is half way across, Jane grabs one of the handrails and starts shaking.

Adams face goes white. "Stop it, Jane!" he yells in a voice a little higher pitched than normal."I swear I'll hit you!"

"Don't be such a baby," Jane says. "I'm just having a bit of fun. You're not going to fall."

Jane steps back and lets Adam wobble his way across. You can see the relief on his face when he reaches solid ground again.

"That wasn't funny. You know I hate heights."

Jane turns her back on Adam to head up the path, but not before you see a little grin cross her face.

Jane is trouble.

You hear the waterfall up ahead. It sounds like someone is running a bath only louder. Then you feel moisture in the air as the wind-blown spray drifts into the jungle.

Jane is the first to see the tumbling mass of white water as she comes around the corner. "Wow! Look at that!"

You nearly bump into her as you take in the scene.

The waterfall is about fifteen feet wide and thirty feet high. It pours over a lip of rock straight out of the jungle into a shimmering pool below. Ferns and palms crowd the stream on both sides. Grey stones cover the bottom of the pool and waves of bright green weed dance in the current.

"Last one in is a monkey's bum!" Jane yells as she runs down the path towards the pool.

Before you know it, Adam has scooted past you and is in hot pursuit of his sister. At the pool's edge Jane throws off her t-shirt and makes a running dive. Adam tosses his phone onto the pile and follows.

Adam is first to surface about half way across the expanse of water. Jane continues to swim underwater, the bright yellow of her swimsuit glowing under the water, until she is nearly under the cascade. When she surfaces her teeth gleam white and her long hair plasters itself to her neck and shoulders.

"I win!" she yells as her fist pumps the air in triumph.

Not bothering to remove your t-shirt, you dive into the pool. The water is cool and refreshing. After paddling to where Jane and Adam are treading water you look down into the depths. "Amazing how clear the water is," you say.

You dive down to see if you can touch the bottom but you're forced to surface again before you get there.

"The water's a lot deeper than it looks," you tell the others when you surface. "I can't reach the bottom."

"Let me have a go," Jane says before flipping over and kicking towards the bottom.

You and Adam watch as she pulls herself deeper and deeper. Before you know it she's holding on to a clump of weed and looking around. After 20 seconds or so, slowly releasing air bubbles as she goes, she rises to the surface.

"Wow you *are* good," you say when her head finally breaks the surface. "You were down there for ages."

Jane has a grin from ear to ear. "And look what I found."

Glinting in the palm of her hand is a small metal cross, like one you'd wear around your neck.

The three of you swim to the pond's edge and sit on a rock.

"Looks like silver," you say, taking the cross and peering at it closely. At the end of each arm is a small hollow. You suspect these would have held precious stones at one time.

On the other side of the cross you see some tiny scratches, but then realize as you inspect them closer they are words etched into the metal. You tilt the cross so the light hits the surface and you can read the words.

"CAROL IIII D.G. 1805," you read. "That sounds vaguely familiar." You're sure you've read seem something similar in one of your treasure hunting books. You hand the cross back to Jane and try to remember what you've read.

With a towel from your daypack you dry your hair, still thinking hard as you do so. "Right, CAROL. If I remember correctly that's Spanish for Charles."

Adam seems interested. "Do you think it came from the treasure ship that went down?"

"It's certainly the right time," you say. "The pirate ship we're looking for was raiding the French and Spanish colonies along the South American coast and then came to this part of the Pacific chasing whales to restock their supply of oil. I wonder if some the treasure was salvaged from the wreck after all."

"We could get some scuba gear from the resort and come back. Maybe there is more stuff at the bottom of the pool," Jane says. "I got my dive ticket last summer in Hawaii."

"That's a good idea. I have my ticket too. The two of us could team up for safety."

You've got to admit that the bottom of a deep pool under a waterfall would be a great place to hide treasure.

"Or we could check out this Smuggler's Cove place first and then decide," Adam said. "It's almost an hour back to the resort." Once again the twins look for you for a decision. The cross was a good find, and the date is certainly from the right era.

Should you check out Smuggler's Cove before going all the way back for scuba gear? Or is the cross an indication that there is more treasure to be found?

It is time to make another decision. Do you:

Carry on to Smuggler's Cove? **P21**

Or

Go back to resort for scuba gear? **P26**

You have decided to carry on to Smuggler's Cove.

As the three of you make your way along the jungle path to Smuggler's Cove, the path twists and turns so much it's hard to know which direction you're heading. The canopy overhead is so dense that in places it feels like evening has come even though your rumbling stomach tells you it is probably closer to lunchtime.

When you come to a large tree that's fallen across the path you stop. "Anyone hungry?" you ask. "Maybe we should have lunch."

Jane and Adam nod their agreement, sit on the tree trunk and rummage through their daypacks.

"I've got a couple of apples and a chocolate energy bar," says Jane.

"Snap," you say, holding up a couple bars of your own. "I love chocolate."

Adam pulls out a bottle of water and packets of cheese and crackers. "I've got heaps of nuts too," he says waving a bulging zip-lock bag. "Sing out if you want some."

As the three of you have lunch you discover that Adam and Jane's parents are both dentists. Jane tells you they're only happy when they're on vacation.

Adam nods. "Nobody is ever happy to see them at work. Their clients are either in pain or unhappy about how much it's going to cost. It's no wonder Mom and Dad are happy to get away from all the grumbling."

You'd never really thought much about the life of dentists. "Still they can afford to buy you the latest phone and take you to nice places so I bet you're not complaining."

Adam shrugs. "I'd rather they were happier sometimes. What's the use of money if you're miserable?"

Jane jumps up and starts closing her bag up. "Let's make them really happy and find some treasure. Then they can retire and be on vacation all the time."

"I'll go along with that," you say as you stand up and get ready to move off.

You and the twins have only gone on a hundred yards or so when a waist-high pile of stones appears about ten paces off the path.

"I wonder who made that cairn?" you say, pushing back fern fronds and making your way through the undergrowth.

The stones have been stacked with care and fit together snugly. On top of the pile is large flat rock overgrown with lichen and moss. The moss is growing in a funny pattern.

You pull your pocket knife out and start scraping the growth off the stone. As you do so, letters are revealed.

"Wow, come look at this," you call out to the others.

Adam and Jane work their way through the greenery and peer down at the characters you've uncovered.

"Does that say 1806?" Jane asks.

The grooves in the rock are shallow. Wind, rain and plant life have pitted the surface over the years but you can still make them out.

"That's the year the ship went down!" you say.

Adams eyes widen. "So the rumors are true."

You can't believe what you're seeing. "It looks that way."

Jane steps back and gives the pile of rocks a quick once-over. "Do you think something is buried here? Treasure maybe?"

You shake your head. "Too obvious I would have thought." Then you have a thought. "Hey, Adam, help me lift the top stone, maybe the cairn is hollow."

You and Adam grab a side of the rock each and hoist it off the pile, flipping it onto the ground as you do so.

"Nope, not hollow," you say. Then you notice more writing on the underside of the rock.

"What's this?" you say, bending down and running your fingers over the surface. "Letters, but they're upside…"

Jane does an excited little hop and says, "*Port-au-Prince*! It says *Port-au-Prince*. Isn't that the ship you told us about?"

"The one and only," you say unable to stop your face from twisting up into a grin.

Adam bends down to stroke the rock. "So it did run aground here on the island."

"Crikey! We're going to be rich!" Jane squeals.

"Not so fast," you say. "The treasure may be here on the island, but we still have to find it."

Adam scratches his head. "So what now?"

You're not quite sure what to do. Why would shipwrecked sailors build a cairn here in the jungle? And why would they put the date on one side and the name of their ship on the other? Could it be a hint as to where the treasure is hidden, or is it a memorial to those lost when the ship sank?

"I think we should carry on to Smuggler's Cove," you say.

With the cairn penciled onto your map, you rejoin the path. You've only walked another mile or so when you hear the faint sound of waves breaking. Minutes later you come upon the rocky shore. To the east, about two hundred yards down the coast, is a small cove protected from the sea by a rocky arm that protrudes out into the ocean. To your surprise, there is a yacht anchored about thirty yards off shore. Sitting on the boat's deck are two men wearing straw hats and floral shirts.

Pulled up on the beach is a small rowboat.

"Get down," you whisper. "Someone's rowed their dinghy ashore, they must be nearby."

Jane's hand rests on your shoulder as she crouches down beside you. "Do you think they're looking for treasure too?" she whispers.

"Let's hope not. But if they are, we don't want them to know they have competition."

"So what do we do?" Adam asks quietly. "What if they're dangerous?"

"We could pretend we're tourists who've come for a swim," Jane says. "I doubt they'd hurt a bunch of kids."

"We *are* tourists silly," Adam says with a hint of sarcasm

in his voice. "We don't need to pretend."

"They won't know we're looking for treasure," Jane says. "And if they are, we might be able to get some valuable information from them."

Suddenly the twins are both looking at you to make a decision. You're not sure what would be the best plan of action. The men on the yacht could be innocent tourists or they could be up to something fishy.

What should you do? Do you:

Watch the yacht from the jungle? **P34**

Or

Pretend you're tourists going for a swim? **P39**

You have decided to go to the resort for scuba gear.

After finding the cross in the pool at the foot of the falls, you want to see if there is more treasure sitting on the bottom. Only Jane is a good enough swimmer to get to the bottom without scuba gear, and even she will tire quickly once she's swum to the bottom a few times.

"Okay, let's get back to the resort and get some gear," you say. "We'll be able to search the whole pool thoroughly that way. Where there's one artifact there might be others."

Everyone has a bounce in their step and talks of what they'll spend their bounty on as the three of you head back to the resort.

The dive shop is tucked around the back and in the basement of the main building. You hire a small tank, regulator, and weight belt, divide the equipment between you, and within fifteen minutes you're trudging back into the jungle towards the waterfall.

The day is heating up and the jungle is humid. Sweat drips down your back. Half an hour later, just as you turn off the main path and head up towards the waterfall, a sudden flurry of wings and bright red bodies flash through the canopy overhead.

"Something's spooked the lorikeets," you say.

You are only a short way up the waterfall track when you hear heavy footsteps crashing through the undergrowth off to your left.

"Quiet, someone's coming," you whisper. "Quick, hide in the ferns. We don't want anyone to know we're here."

The three of you burrow into a mass of fronds beside the path and wait. The footsteps get closer and louder. Someone is breathing hard, like they've been running.

Then, through a gap in the ferns, you see a man carrying a wire cage full of lorikeets.

"Don't move," you whisper to the others.

When the sound of the man's footsteps has passed, you climb out of your hiding spot.

"Did you see the cage full of birds?" you ask Adam and Jane. "He's been trapping. That'll be what scared the lorikeets a few moments ago."

Adam's face twists into a frown. "Surely that's illegal."

You leaf through your guidebook. "You're right, the book says the birds are protected."

"We need to do something," Jane says.

"But what?" you say. "This island's miles from anywhere."

Adam pulls out his cell phone. "We may not have a signal, but my phone still works as a camera. I should take some video so we have something to show the authorities."

Jane nods her agreement. "Let's leave the scuba gear here and follow him. If we get some pictures the police on the mainland might be able to identify them."

Their plan sounds dangerous, especially if the poachers see you taking photos. But you agree with the twins. You can't let some greedy idiot get away with poaching protected birds.

"Okay," you say. "But we'll need to be careful. Bird smuggling is big business and poachers are dangerous. Who knows what he'll do if he catches us spying. He might even be armed so keep quiet and no talking."

That said, you push the scuba gear under a fern and break one of the fronds so you'll know where it is when you come back. Then you pick up your daypack and start moving down the track.

You are confident of catching up with the man carrying the heavy cage so you don't rush. Instead you walk quietly and hope that you see him before he sees you.

When you get back to the junction where the waterfall track meets the main path you stop.

"Which way?" Jane asks.

You think a moment. "I can't imagine him going towards the resort."

"I agree," Adam says. "He must be heading towards the cove."

It isn't long before you see a flash of color ahead of you.

You signal to the others and come to a stop. "There he is," you whisper. "Let's keep pace with him and see where he goes."

Fifteen minutes later Jane tilts her head and cups a hand around an ear. "I think I hear the ocean. Maybe he has a boat."

"Okay, easy now," you say. "We don't want him to spot us."

As you move along the path, the sound of the waves gets louder. Coconut palms start to appear amongst the ferns and other broad-leafed plants, and after another fifty yards you see the ocean through a gap in the trees.

When you reach the edge of the jungle you stop. The man is walking along the shore towards a dinghy pulled up onto the rocky beach a hundred yards away. In the sparkling blue water of the cove, a single-masted yacht rocks gently at anchor. Two men sit on deck drinking beer.

"Welcome to Smuggler's Cove," you say.

"So what now?" Adam asks.

"Follow me," you say. "And keep low."

You step back into the jungle. Jane and Adam follow as you walk parallel to the beach in the direction of the yacht. The ground is sandy here and the shrubs and ferns less dense so the going is relatively easy while still giving you cover from the men on the boat.

When you think you've gone far enough, you creep back towards the beach along what looks like a natural watercourse. The twins follow close behind.

But just as the clear waters of Smuggler's Cove appear before you, your feet are whipped out from under you and you're hoisted into the air.

"Yow!" Jane yelps in surprise.

"Ouch," Adam says. "Someone's squashing my legs."

The more you squirm, the tighter the net pulls around you, squashing the three of you together. Your arms are pressed to your body and Adam's weight pins you against the mesh.

"What now?" Adam grunts. "Any other bright ideas from our expedition leader?"

Jane's foot is pressed against the side of your face. You can see the ground about three feet below you. The net rocks back and forth like a hammock.

"I've got a knife in the side pouch of my daypack. Can anyone reach it?" you say.

"I think … I think I can," Jane says, contorting limbs.

You hear Jane breathing hard with effort and then feel a tugging on your pack.

"Can you move to your right?" she asks.

"I'll try," you say, pressing hard with your elbows while rotating your body at the same time.

"Okay, that should do it."

With your face pressed hard to the mesh you roll your eyes and try to see what is happening on the beach. Did the men on the boat hear the *twang* as the trap went off? Are they coming?

"Got it!" Jane says.

"Well, start cutting," you urge her. "Quickly, in case the men heard us."

"Watch it with that knife Sis," Adam says. "You nearly got my leg there."

"Sorry," Jane says, hacking a little more carefully.

You can feel the net stretch as Jane cuts at it and you sink closer and closer to the ground as each minute goes by. Then, like a zipper opening, the net splits apart in a rush and dumps you on the ground.

"Oooof!" you grunt as Adam lands on top of you.

Adam rolls away and you get onto your knees and look around. Two men in flora shirts are moving up the beach towards your position.

"They've seen us!" you say. "We need to get out of here."

"I'm still caught up!" Jane says, kicking her foot like she's trying to shake off her shoe.

You hear panic in her voice. When you look over, you see that a section of net has become entangled around her foot.

"Quick, give me the knife! Stay still." You start hacking at the strands holding her foot. "Get ready to run the moment you're free."

Adam has his camera out and is taking shots of the men coming towards you.

"Hey you!" one of the men shouts. "What are you doing with that camera?"

"Hurry up!" Adam says. "They're nearly here."

"Go," Jane says. "Save yourselves."

With one final slice of the net, Jane pulls her foot free and scrabbles to her feet.

"Split up and run," you say, taking off back the way you came. "Meet you where we left the scuba gear."

With that, the three of you plunge into the jungle running for all you're worth. You duck and weave around trees and shrubs, barging through clumps of fern and eventually come to rest at the base of a large tree. Breathing hard, you stop to catch your breath and listen for footsteps.

Then you hear Adam's voice. "Let me go!"

As you suck in air, your heart pounds. The men must have gone for Adam because he had the camera. You wonder if Jane got away or has suffered the same fate?

"If you kids tell anyone, your friend is toast!" of the men yells into the jungle.

They sound so angry, but what can you do? Luckily the contour of the land gives you a hint as to where you are. You head down a slight slope hoping to cross the waterfall track, pulling the greenery back as you go. Every few minutes you stop, duck down and listen for footsteps. Finally you find the track you're looking for and a couple hundred meters up the trail you see the broken fern frond.

You tuck yourself deep into the ferns and wait to see if Jane turns up. As you wait you inspect the underside of the nearest frond. Two rows of little brown dots run in down each side of the leaf's finger-sized offshoots. These are the spores that will be blown into the wind and grow into more ferns when the conditions are right. You must remember to tell Adam all about them when you see him next. If you see him again, that is.

Fifteen minutes later you hear the crunch of footsteps.

You lean back deeper into the greenery and hope that it's Jane and not one of the men. Then you hear a voice.

"Helloooo. Anyone here?" It's Jane looking for the spot where you stashed the scuba gear.

You crawl out from your hiding place and stand up, looking around as you do so. When you catch Jane's eye your put one finger to your lips and wave her over."Shush… The poachers might still be around."

Jane comes over and the two of you duck back under cover.

"Did you see them get Adam?" you whisper.

Jane shakes her head. "I heard him yell, but kept going. I didn't see any point in both of us getting caught."

"So what do we do now? Do we try and save Adam ourselves or go for help?"

"I don't know. I'm afraid they might hurt him."

"Don't worry, we'll work something out," you say.

You think hard. What should you do? Going back for help will take time. Do you have that luxury? What if the poachers take off with Adam in their boat? You may never see him again. But how will two kids be able to handle evil poachers?

It is time to make an important decision. Do you:

Try to help Adam? **P62**

Or

Go back to the resort for help? **P78**

You have decided to watch the yacht from the jungle.

The three of you sneak back to the cover of the jungle and creep silently towards the cove.

"Stay in single file," you whisper, "and watch where you step so we don't make too much noise."

Jane suppresses a giggle and falls in behind. "It's like we're ninja spies."

You carefully pull the shrubbery aside so it doesn't snap back in Jane's face and work your way closer to the yacht.

"I hope you know what you're doing," Adam whispers, bringing up the rear. "What if they catch us spying on them?"

You put your index finger up to your lip. "Quiet… If you guys keep talking they'll hear us for sure."

The ground is sandy underfoot. Flowering shrubs crowd one another and the going is slow. Bees hum from flower to flower collecting nectar. After a few minutes, you've worked your way to a spot just inland from where the yacht is anchored. The beach slopes steeply towards the water and unlike the white sand, made from ground shells, on the lagoon side of the island, the sand here is course, dark and volcanic in origin. The men's voices can be heard talking and laughing over the slap of the waves.

You signal the others to get down and crawl towards the beach on hands and knees. From under a bush, you get a better view of what the men are doing. Jane and Adam follow your lead.

The three of you peer carefully through the lower branches. The men are close. The two on deck keep looking towards shore, obviously waiting for whoever is on shore to return.

"What are they doing?" Jane whispers close to your ear.

You look at her sternly and move your hand across your lips in a zipping motion. The last thing you want is for the men to hear you.

Black lettering graces the side of the boat's hull. *Moneymaker* it says. That sounds like the name of a treasure hunter's ship if ever you've heard one.

A moment later there is whistling in the jungle behind you. You drop flat and hope whoever it is doesn't see you. The sound is ten yards to your right and moving towards the beach.

When you sneak a glance, you see a man with a cage full of brightly colored bird walking towards the dingy.

Holding the cage in one hand, the man drags the small boat into water. He stows the cage in the front of the boat, climbs aboard and slots the oars into the rowlocks. The man's rowing technique is good. It doesn't take him long to cross the short distance to the yacht.

"Traps are working well," he calls up to the men on deck. "Here grab this rope and get ready, I'll pass the cage up."

With a heave, the man raises the metal cage above his head where it is grabbed by one of the men. The man on deck swings the cage over the railing and is about to lower it, when he screams out and drops the cage with a thump.

"Ouch! Filthy bird just took a hunk out of my hand!" he howls waving his hand in the air.

The other men laugh at their companion's misfortune. "I've told you before to watch out. Their beaks can take your finger right off if they get hold of it properly."

The hurt man tucks his injured hand under his armpit and paces around the deck for a moment, grumbling and cursing under his breath before coming back to kick the cage. "Watch it you horrible birds. Next time I'll drop you overboard!"

"Horrible birds," a parrot mimics. "Horrible birds. Horrible birds."

The two men laugh again. "Those birds are smarter than you are Jimmy. Maybe we should drop *you* overboard."

The man in the dinghy chuckles again and then grabs the railing and slides the dinghy through the water to the stern of the yacht. He climbs up a short ladder and secures the dinghy's painter to a cleat on deck.

"Another day, another dollar," one of the men says. "It always amazes me what people will pay for exotic birds."

As the men start preparing the yacht for departure, the man with the sore hand moves to the cockpit. He turns the key to start the diesel engine and with a puff of smoke the engine rumbles into life. The man checks that water is coming from the exhaust port in the transom and then waits by the wheel.

The other two go to the bow ready to pull up the anchor. The man behind the wheel inches the yacht forward.

The men on the bow are talking, but the throb of the yacht's motor drowns out their voices.

"Poachers," you say to the twins. "The lowest of the low."

"Poor birds. What will happen to them?" Jane asks.

"Life in cages." Adam looks angry and starts to say something else, but then clamps his jaw closed and growls like a dog protecting his territory. His face is red and his clenched fists shake.

"Don't blow a foo-foo valve little brother," Jane says. "Adam works at the animal shelter as a volunteer," she says to you."He gets so angry when he sees animals being mistreated."

"With good reason," you say. "But what do we do about it?"

"We need to tell the authorities," Adam says. "That's what we do."

"But we're already here, we may as well have a look around," Jane says. "The poachers are leaving. It will be a wasted trip otherwise."

The twins look to you. You could go back to the resort, but would the resort's management do anything? And Jane has a point about your trek being wasted if you go straight back to the resort.

You scratch your head and think. Both options have merit. It is time to make a decision. Do you:

Go back to the resort and report the poachers? **P46**

Or

Have a look around Smugglers Cove? **P54**

You have decided to pretend you are tourists going for a swim.

"If we're going to do this," you say, "we've got to get our story straight."

Jane smiles at your decision. "I read somewhere that it's best to tell as much of the truth as possible when undercover, there's less things to remember that way."

"Okay, let's go for a swim and see if they approach us. If the men are tourists they'll most likely say hello."

"And if not," Adam buts in, "they'll try to scare us off."

"Exactly!" Jane says.

"Whatever you do, don't mention treasure," you say. "If we ask too many questions they'll get suspicious."

With that, Jane pulls her towel out of her pack and walks calmly out of hiding and on to the stony beach. You and Adam, now committed to the plan, follow her lead.

You keep your head down, as if watching your step as you walk, but your eyes dart up every few seconds to see what the men's reaction is to your arrival. One of the men sees you and nudges the other with his foot. The other man is less subtle and stares a little too long, his smile turning down a little too quickly.

"They don't look pleased to see us," you whisper. "Keep moving, but get ready to scarper in a hurry."

Jane's acting skills are quite convincing. She skips on to the beach and, a short distance from the dingy, lays out her towel. "I'm going for a swim," she announces loud enough to carry to the men onboard the yacht."

You bend down to lay out your towel and whisper to Adam, "One of us should stay on the beach and keep an eye out for the shore party."

"I'm not a great swimmer," Adam says. "I don't mind staying."

"I might go for a quick snorkel and have a look around then," you say.

Jane hits the water then turns and calls out, "The water's so warm!"

With your mask and flippers in your hand you walk to the water's edge. After rinsing your mask you slip the rubber strap over your head and sit in the coarse sand to put on your flippers. Then lifting your feet high, you walk backwards into the water.

Jane is right, the water is warm. You've only just started snorkeling when you hear Adam yell.

"Hey! What do you think you're doing?"

Jane has heard him too and is staring past you towards the beach.

You turn around to see what has got Adam so excited.

A man, carrying a cage of brightly colored birds has come out of the jungle and is making his way along the beach towards the dinghy.

By now, Jane is swimming back to shore. When she reaches your position she says, "These guys are trapping birds. Adam's a fanatic when it comes to animal welfare. I hope he doesn't do something stupid."

"Me too."

By now, Adam is up off his towel and marching towards the man carrying the cage. The men on the yacht have seen him too.

"Quick," Jane says. "He's going to nut-off at this guy. We need to stop him."

"And fast," you say. "That man could get violent."

As the two of you race back to shore you watch Adam. He's marching towards the man with the cages like a zealot on a mission, his vision focused straight ahead, his arms pumping.

The man sees Adam coming at him and puts his hands on his hips, seemingly unconcerned about the angry boy striding towards him.

You can't help admire Adam's courage as you hit the beach.

When Adam speaks, you can hear every word.

"These birds are protected you brain-dead imbecile!" he yells. "Let them go or I'll report you to the authorities!"

"Subtle, your brother," you say to Jane.

Adam, although brave, is being guided by his heart and not his head. You're not quite sure what he expects to achieve. Does Adam really think this criminal is going to take any notice of a kid?

"Who are you to tell me what to do?" the man says. "You

tourists think you run things now?"

But Adam isn't listening. He's had a rush of blood to his head, his face has gone scarlet in rage and he's not thinking straight.

"I'll see you in jail!" Adam yells, spittle flying. Then he looks over at the men on the yacht. "I'll see you all in jail!" Without warning, Adam runs at the man on the beach and pushes him hard in the chest.

The man, standing with feet spread in front of the cage, loses his balance and tumbles back, trips over the cage and falls awkwardly on the ground.

In a flash, Adam reaches down and unhooks the top of the cage. In a blur of color the dozen or so lorikeets fly off into the jungle.

"Why you little brat," the man growls from the ground. "Those birds were worth hundreds of dollars."

Thankfully, you and Jane have reached the scene.

"Adam, let's go." You grab Adam's arm but he stands fast. "Adam, I said it's time to go."

The man snarls like a wounded animal and lurches to his feet.

"Run Adam!" Jane yells.

Adam sees the man coming at him with fists clenched and finally realizes how furious he is.

You hear splashes and cast a glance towards the boat. The two other men are swimming strongly towards the shore. They will be here in a moment.

But Adam is too slow and the man's meaty hand clamps around his forearm.

"I'll teach you a lesson you little rat bag!"

Jane takes a couple steps forward and kicks the man in the kneecap.

"Ouch!"

It's not a crippling blow, but it's enough of a distraction for Adam to break the man's grip.

"Run!" Jane yells again.

The other men have reached the beach and are sprinting towards you.

"Now!" you scream once more, tugging at Adam's arm.

Jane needs no prompting. In a flash she heads back toward the pile of gear on the sand, scoops up her daypack and scurries into the jungle. You and Adam are twenty yards behind her.

As you hit the track leading inland there is a thud and a grunt behind you. Without even turning, you know Adam has fallen. When you spin around for confirmation, you see one of the men from the yacht is nearly upon him. "Go!" Adam says, his eyes pleading. "Go get help!"

You want to help, but it's too late. Adam is right. There is nothing to be gained by both of you being captured. You take off, casting a quick glance over your shoulder as you enter the jungle.

The man has hold of Adam's arm and is dragging him back towards the beach. Once you're twenty yards along the path and out of their view, you duck into some ferns and watch through the fronds. The second man from the boat is out of shape. The swim and the run have sapped his energy. When he sees that his friend has captured Adam, he bends over, puts his hands on his knees and gasps for air.

The man that Jane kicked in the knee is last to arrive. He hobbles over and glares at Adam, then yells into the jungle. "Hey brats, if you don't want your friend hurt you'd better keep you're your mouths shut!"

And with that, two of the men force Adam into the dinghy and start rowing back towards their boat. The other picks up the empty cage and heads a hundred yards or so further down the beach and then turns and walks back into the jungle.

"Jane?" you call out. "Can you hear me?"

You climb out of your hiding spot and start down the path towards the resort, hoping to come across Jane. It isn't long before you hear a rustle of leaves in the canopy.

"Jane?"

Chimpanzee noises come from a tree branch above you and you catch a flash of yellow. "Jane, come down. They've got Adam."

Within 30 seconds, Jane is back on the ground. "Is he okay?"

"I don't know. Did you hear them yell out that we'd better keep quiet?"

Jane shakes her head. "What do we do?"

"We either try to help Adam, or go back to the resort I suppose."But you're not sure. What should you do?

It is time to make a decision. Do you:

Try to help Adam? **P62**

Or

Go back to the resort for help? **P78**

You have decided to go back and report the poachers.

You can't help agreeing with Adam. Unless you report the poachers right away they could disappear before the authorities have a chance to locate them. There are so many yachts cruising the South Pacific islands this time of year, a few hours could make all the difference.

"We'd better get back to the resort pronto," you say, doing some quick calculations in your head. "If we move fast, we'll be back in an hour. If that yacht is traveling at 8 knots, every hour that goes by the authorities will have another um ... 250 square miles to search."

Jane looks surprised."How did you figure that out so quickly?"

[If you are interested in finding out how the math works, turn to **P134** - if not continue reading.]

You start down the path back towards the resort. You hear the twin's footsteps behind you. Jane mumbles numbers as you half walk, half jog through the jungle.

You've hardly had time to build up a sweat when you see something that looks like a huge spider's web off to your left. You signal a halt and point at whatever it is hanging in the trees. "What's that?"

Adam takes a step forward. "A bird net, I think. Those poachers must plan on coming back for more. I bet they anchor in the safety of the lagoon tonight and come back tomorrow."

You shrug. "It's possible I suppose."

The net is positioned in such a way that that you hadn't noticed it before. The fine mesh, barely visible in the shade of the jungle canopy, stretches between two trees. The net hangs loose and there is already a parrot struggling in its mesh.

The trapped parrot squawks and flaps uselessly.

Adam is first to rush forward. "Have you got a knife?"

You think about Adam's comment about the poachers 'coming back' as you fish your pocket knife out of your daypack.

"Careful with the pressure you put on the net," Adam warns. "The fine bones in their wings are extremely fragile."

Adam holds the frightened bird still as you cut the strands of nylon holding it. The mesh, though fine, is as strong as fishing line. After a few minutes the last of the net falls away. Adam holds the bird in his outstretched arms and lets it go. With a squawk and a series of rapid wing beats the bird darts off to join his flock in the jungle.

"We should take the net back as evidence," Jane says. "The authorities may not believe us otherwise."

"Jane's right," you say. "I'll cut it down."

Five minutes later the net is bundled up in your daypack and the three of you are back on the path towards the resort.

"I wonder how many more of those awful nets they have

strung up around the island," Adam says. "And how many poor birds they've captured."

"Don't worry, Adam," Jane says. "Once we report them, I'm sure the authorities will put an end to their operation."

"They'd better," Adam says. "Otherwise I'll sink their boat."

"How will you do that?" you ask. "Got a torpedo hidden in your luggage?"

"No, but I bet I can find a drill at the resort," Adam says, his voice sounding serious. "It doesn't take a very big leak to fill a boat with water."

Jane looks at her brother. "Let's hope it doesn't come to that."

"Enough talk about sinking boats," you say. "Save your breath for the trip back."

With that you start jogging. Within minutes sweat is dripping from your forehead and down your back. The twins puff along behind you.

When the first of the resort's outbuildings appear, you slow to a walk and pull the water bottle out of your pack. Its contents are warm, but at least they're wet.

"So who do we report the poachers to?" Jane asks.

You turn your palms upward and shrug. "That's the problem isn't it? Who can we trust?"

Jane gives you a curious look. "You don't trust the resort management? Do you think they're in on it?"

"They could be," Adam says. "It's hard to believe

nobody's noticed nets before, but what choice do we have?"

"Adam's right," you say. "There aren't any police on the island, so management's the closest thing to authority there is around here."

"Unless we can contact the police directly," Jane says.

"How would we do that?" Adam says.

Jane gives her brother a cheeky grin. "Sneak into the office and use their phone. Who needs to know?"

Jane has a point. If someone at the resort is involved, telling them what you've discovered would only give the poachers time to retrieve their nets and flee. It could also be dangerous for you and the twins. Criminals don't like it when people interfere with their cash flow.

You're not sure Jane's plan is a good one. Adam's not looking too convinced either.

"Oh come on you two," Jane says. "Embrace your inner ninja!"

"Let's check the office before we make a decision," you say. "See if it's even possible."

Adam reluctantly agrees.

"Yippee, it's ninja spy time." Jane announces gleefully, about to set off.

"Wait," you say, grabbing her arm. "We need a plan, Miss Ninja."

After some discussion, the three of you decide that Jane, using her acting skills, will distract whoever is on the main desk, while you and Adam scope out the phone situation in the office next door.

"Right, can I go now?" Jane asks, keen to begin her role.

You look toward Adam, who nods his agreement. "Right," you say. "Let's do this."

Jane skips towards the main entrance and the reception desk beyond, while you and Adam walk around to the side door.

"Let's give Jane a minute before we go in," you say. "If we keep near the back wall of the lobby and walk quietly, we should be able to make it to the office without anyone at the main desk seeing us."

When you reach the side door, you can already hear Jane's voice. She's speaking to a middle-aged man in a floral shirt behind the desk.

"So what fishing charters do you offer?"

As the man lays a number of brochures on the counter and explains the times and costs of each option, Jane continues her act.

It's time for you and Adam to make your move.

When Jane sees you enter, she moves along the counter a little more so that, as the man follows her, his back is turned towards you and Adam.

It's only twenty paces to the office and you cover the ground quickly. Thankfully, the office door is open. You cross your fingers and hope it is empty, but unfortunately, as you get closer, you hear a man's voice.

"How many birds?" the voice in the office says. "Forty?

Great."

You and Adam freeze, your backs to the wall next to the office door. You hear the crackle of a VHF radio and a male voice, but can't quite make out the words.

Then the man in the office speaks again. "Great ... Yeah ... I've got the buyer lined up."

"He must be talking to the poachers," you whisper in Adam's ear.

"Bring the yacht into the lagoon. Just make sure you keep the cages below deck so the tourists don't get a look."

Adam's jaw is clenched, his face turning red. You're afraid he's about to storm into the office so you grab his arm and drag him back to the side door and out into the garden.

Once outside, you guide him onto a bench and sit down beside him. "Easy does it. You can't rush in there and confront the guy. You've got no proof, and no backup. What are you going to do, lock him in your family's bungalow until the police arrive? Duh, I don't think so."

"But..."

"Think," you say softly, hoping to calm Adam down."We need a plan if we're going to stop these guys. You *do* want to stop them don't you?"

"Well sure but..."

"Right then let's use our heads and do this right. Too many crooks have gotten off because someone's gone off half cocked and blown the investigation."

You can see the tension leaving Adam's face as he realizes

you're on his side.

"Yeah okay," he says. "I suppose you're right."

Moments later Jane arrives. "Why'd you come outside?"

You explain about the conversation you've overheard.

"So they *are* in on it," Jane says. "What now?"

"There are phones in the rooms," Adam says. "Let's use those."

You shake your head. "We can't. You've got to get reception to put you through to the number you want. They'll want to know why you're asking to be connected to the police or wildlife rangers. There must be another way."

Adam stands and places his hands on his hips. "Well if they're bringing their boat to the lagoon, I say we find a way to free the birds and sink it. That'll teach them a lesson."

"Yeah, let's sink their boat!" Jane says hopping up and down eagerly. "Underwater attack of the ninjas!"

"Are you serious?" you say, wondering what has gotten into these two. "Do you have any idea what would happen if we got caught?"

But Adam's eyes have glazed over. In his mind he's already planning his assault.

You shake his arm. "Are you listening to me?"

Adam comes out of his trance and glares at you. "Well I'm going to do it with or without your help. I don't care if I get caught!"

"What do you suggest?" Jane asks, staring at you. "Got a better plan?"

There is nothing you'd like more than seeing the poachers yacht on the bottom of the lagoon. It would certainly put a halt to their operation. But if you get caught, who knows what the poachers will do.

It's not an easy decision to make, but time is running out. Do you:

Try to sink the poacher's boat? **P114**

Or

Try to find some other way to contact the authorities? **P126**

You have decided to look around Smuggler's Cove.

You've come this far so you don't see any harm in having a look around Smuggler's Cove while you're here. "A quick snorkel to see if it's worth coming back, then we'll go report the poachers. What do you say?"

The twins seem happy with this compromise.

The beach on this side of the island is steep and the sand is dark from the island's many volcanic eruptions over the centuries, unlike the white sand of the lagoon beach. No reef means this part of the coast is open to whatever the Pacific throws at it. If it weren't for the cove being sheltered by a rocky point, snorkeling would be difficult except in the best of weather.

As the smuggler's yacht disappears around the point, the three of you come out of the jungle and make your way down to the water's edge. You stick in a toe. The water is warm and inviting.

You pull out your mask and flippers. "I'm going in."

The twins are quick to get their flippers on.

Within minutes the three of you are floating on the surface looking down into a wonderland of gently swaying aquatic plants and interesting sea creatures.

You veer left to inspect the western side of the cove. This side is a little more exposed to the wind. You figure if something was to wash ashore, it's more likely to end up on this side of the cove.

At first the water in the cove is reasonably shallow. You can see the bottom as clear as if you were in a swimming pool. Blue fish dart left and right. Anemones, their tentacles waving, do their dance in the current.

You wonder if there are giant squid in these waters. Probably not you figure, they tend to hang around where waters are colder and deeper.

You are pleased the weather is calm and the waves slight. This coast would be treacherous in a storm. It's easy to imagine how a sailing ship could run aground in a spot like this.

As you kick your flippers, you glide along the surface and your head sweeps back and forth scanning the bottom for any sign of wreckage. Various corals, orange and purple starfish, sponges and crabs cover the rocky bottom along with a multitude of empty shells. Brightly colored fish dart this way and that.

When a large moray eel poke its head out of a crack in the rocks and stares up at you, his sharp teeth glistening in his partly open mouth, you kick a little harder. Morays are not a creature you want to tangle with and this one looks hungry.

After about 15 minutes you stick your head out of the water. Where have the twins gone? At first you can't see them. Then there is a splash as Jane's head breaks the surface. Adam surfaces a split second later.

You pull off your mask and spit out your snorkel. "See anything?"

Both of them shake their heads.

"Okay well let's give it another few minutes and then head back."

The twins give you a thumbs-up and resume their search.

As you move further from shore, the water gets deeper and a sheer wall of rock plunges into the blue. On this wall grows an underwater jungle of marine life.

You feel the ocean swell lift you gently as you stare at the beauty below. When a big flash of silver appears out of nowhere, you jerk with fright thinking it's a shark, but then the mass breaks up into thousands of smaller units and you realize it's only a school of fish.

Where did they come from? The rock wall looks solid all the way down, but there must be a passage or something you can't see from the surface. Once you heart rate returns to normal you take a deep breath and dive.

As you descend you see the wall has an overhang. Below this protrusion, hidden from the surface, the dark mouth of a cave beckons. Thriving in the cracks around the entrance, are a number of red lobsters, their eyes moving back and forth at the end of spindly stalks as they watch your every move.

You grab the flashlight strapped to your leg and shine its narrow beam into the opening. The light only reaches about ten yards into the cave but it's enough for you to see an old anchor covered in barnacles up against one wall. Could this anchor be from the pirate ship that ran aground all those years ago?

In desperate need of air, you kick for the surface, angling out from under the overhand as you rise. When your head breaks the surface you spit out your snorkel and suck in a deep breath of warm tropical air. Your heart jumps around in your chest. If there's an anchor here, maybe treasure isn't that far away.

You pull off your mask and look around for the others. When you see them off to your right you wave and yell out. "Quick! Come over here!"

Jane reaches you first."What is it?" she asks as she treads water beside you.

"There's an old anchor in a cave about 10 feet down."

Adam's heard you too. "Could it be from the pirate ship?"

"It's looks about the right size and shape."

"We really need scuba gear if we're going to be exploring caves," Jane says.

"But how will we find the right place again?" Adam asks.

You look towards the beach and then out towards the point near the entrance to Smugglers Cove. "We need to find reference points and line them up," you say. "See that palm with the crooked trunk on the beach? We're in line with that and the top of the volcano behind it." You spin around and point towards the rocky coastline to the west. "And we're about thirty yards from shore. See that unusual rock with the narrow pointy top?"

"So," Jane says, "when we come back, we line up the funny palm tree, the volcano, and that pointy rock, and we'll be in the right spot?"

"Near enough," you say. "Shall we go get some tanks?"

"In a minute," Jane says. "I want to have a quick look first."

You pass your flashlight to Jane. "Here take this and be careful. I wouldn't recommend going inside. The currents are strong and unpredictable around here."

Jane takes a couple deep breaths, flips her feet into the air and dives headlong into the blue. You hold your mask to your face so you can watch as she kicks her way down.

Then with a big kick, the rest of her body disappears.

You lift you head out of the water and look towards Adam. "I hope that crazy sister of yours doesn't go inside."

Adam shrugs. "What can I say? She thinks she's bulletproof."

With a splash your mask hits the water again. There is still no sign of Jane and it already feels like she's been down there for ages. Has she got stuck? Should you dive down to help?

You start taking a series of deep breaths in preparation to dive when a mop of blonde hair floats out from under the overhang. It's Jane and she's kicking hard for the surface.

Moments later she spits out her mouthpiece and takes a breath. You are about to tell her how reckless she's been when she holds out her hand. On her palm is a triangular wedge of silver.

You carefully pick up the piece and hold it closer to your face. "It's part of a coin," you tell the twins.

"Part of a coin?" Adam asks. "What happened to the rest of it?"

"In the old days, when they didn't have the right change, they'd chop coins into smaller pieces." You turn the piece over. Along one edge are three letters, a C, an A and an R. "I bet this once said Carolus. That's Charles in English. King Carolus the fourth ruled Spain in the late 1700 and early 1800s."

Jane's grin gets even bigger. "That date fits with your wreck doesn't it?"

You nod. "Historians think the *Port-au-Prince* went down in the early 1800s but coins last hundreds of years so this certainly could have come from the ship we're after. Fingers crossed we can find some more."

"I didn't go in very far," Jane says, "so I couldn't see much. But how could treasure have ended up in the cave?"

"Storms on an exposed coast like this can really toss things around."

Adam is listening intently to your exchange. "Well let's go get some scuba gear so we can check it out."

The three of you are deep in thought as you make your way back to the beach. Within ten minutes your gear has dried in the sun and you pack up and start back along the track to the resort.

By the time the first of the resort buildings comes into view, you've been walking for over an hour and your legs are tired.

The three of you sit on a low stone wall by the pool and discuss what to do next.

"I'm for getting back to the cove," Jane says. "I need treasure!"

"We *need* to report the poachers first," Adam says.

"But who can we trust?" Jane says. "What if the poachers are working with someone from the resort?"

Jane has a point. What if reporting the poachers to the management ends up warning them?

Maybe you should gather more evidence before you do anything. And, if you do decide to report them, what happens if the authorities stake out the cove? How will you secretly investigate the cave and find treasure with people lurking about?

Adam stands up. "I've been thinking on the walk back and I reckon there's a good chance the poachers will sail in to the lagoon and anchor overnight. It's the only real anchorage on the island. When they do, I'm going to find some way to sink their boat."

"Brilliant," Jane says. "My brother the eco-warrior against three hardened criminals. Good luck with that, sport."

"But what if they don't come here?" you ask.

"I bet they do," Adam says with a serious look on his face. "In fact I'll bet you ice cream for a week they do."

"Well if they do, and that's a big if," Jane says. "I think we should report them and then get back to treasure hunting. We're not even citizens of this country."

You're not quite sure what you think. You'd love to sink the poacher's boat and put them out of action. But Jane has a point. Is it even your fight? And besides, what can three kids do against dangerous men?

Then you have an idea. "Maybe we can bypass the resort management and contact the authorities directly."

Adam frowns. "Well I'm waiting for the boat. I'll sink them even if I have to do it alone."

It's time to make a decision. Do you:

Agree with Adam and try to sink the poacher's boat if they turn up? **P114**

Or

Try to contact the authorities? **P126**

You have decided to try and help Adam.

"Okay, let's see if we can find Adam," you say to Jane. "I don't think we have enough time to go all the way back to the resort for help."

Jane climbs out of the ferns. "So what do we do?"

"We'll have to be stealthy as ninjas, sneak up on them, free Adam, and then get away." You give Jane a big smile. "What could go wrong?"

Jane grins back. "I can think of a few things, but let's not worry about that now. Let's go get my brother."

"First, we'll need camouflage," you say. "Break off some fronds and tie them around your waist with vines. Have them pointing up like a real ferns, that way when we stand still, we'll blend right in with the jungle."

"I've seen movies where commandos rub dirt on their faces," Jane says. "Maybe we should do that too?"

"Good idea," you say. You dig your fingers under the leaf litter at your feet. "The ground is damp under the leaves. Should smear just fine."

Despite the seriousness of the mission you are about to undertake, the two of you can't help laughing a little as you cover your arms, hair and faces. When the two of you have finished, you can barely recognize Jane. She looks half plant, half wild animal.

"Perfect," you say. "Let's go."

You take it slowly in case the poachers have posted a

lookout. Every twenty yards or so you stop, stand perfectly still and listen for footsteps. When you see a flash of color, you stop so abruptly. Jane bumps into your back.

"Shhh... I see one of them."

"Where?" Jane whispers back.

You lift your arm and point to a spot 100 yards or so ahead. The man is leaning against a tree. He has a cigarette in one hand and a walkie-talkie in the other. As you stand there pretending to be a fern, you think about what should be your next step.

The man is too big. How can the two of you possibly subdue him?

You look around at your feet. "No rocks, the soil's soft here," you say."We need a weapon of some sort."

Jane digs a hand into her pocket. "I have something that might help."

"What's that?"

She removes a small bundle of nylon netting. All scrunched up, it looks quite small, but as she spreads the net out, your see it's bigger than you first thought. You stand on one side and give the net a sharp tug. The thin, clear filament is deceptively strong.

"I saw it lying just off the path a while ago and picked it up so some poor animal didn't get tangled up in it." Jane says.

"Good thing you did. At least now we've got something to work with."

After thinking for another few moments, you come up with a plan. "If we secure this piece of net between two trees, we might be able to get the man to run into it and tangle himself him up. Then we can pounce on him, tie him up with vines, and he'll be our prisoner."

"But how do we get him to run into the net?" Jane asks.

"Bait. Once we rig it up, you attract the poacher's attention and then lead him to our trap. Then we pounce."

Jane tilts her head to one side and then back to the other, considering what you've said. "Might work. But what then?"

"Prisoner exchange. We use his walkie-talkie to negotiate with the guys on the boat."

You know the plan has risks, but it's the only one you can think of. If Jane agrees, you'll need to set the trap fast. If the man leaves the jungle and goes back to the boat, your opportunity will be gone.

"Dealing with one man at a time is our only chance, Jane."

She exhales a long sigh, looks around the jungle as if she's trying to come up with an alternative, then turns back to you. "Okay, let's do it."

Thankfully there are vines everywhere and your pocket knife is sharp. You and Jane move back along the path a bit and then work quickly cutting lengths of vine and weaving them through the sides of the net.

Then the net is tied to saplings on either side of the track. These small trees should give way when the man's weight hits, bend inward and add to the tangle. Extra lassos of vine are piled up near the trap for quick use. As an added measure, another length of vine is strung across the path at ankle level, a yard or so before the net, to trip the man up and send him flying headlong into your trap. When you stand back to survey your handiwork, the trap is almost invisible.

"Okay," you say. "We've only got one chance at this. If the man looks like he's getting free, run for it. We'll meet back at the resort."

Jane gulps. You can see her hands are a little shaky. But then so are yours.

"Right, now we need to attract his attention. Take off your camouflage and stand on the far side of the net. Here, use some water from my drink bottle to wash some of that mud off you. Otherwise he'll think you're a member of some long lost tribe."

Jane takes your bottle and squirts water over her face and hair.

"Remember, keep the net between you and him at all times."

Jane wipes her face on her t-shirt. "Okay got it."

As Jane stands in position, ready to act as decoy, you walk closer to where the man is standing and move a few steps off the path. Your camouflage gives you a view through its fronds. When you're near enough that you think the man will hear, you grab a dry branch and snap it sharply in two.

The crack is like a rifle shot in the stillness of the jungle. When a flock of lorikeets takes off from the canopy above you, you duck down, hoping your camouflage is up to the task.

It isn't long before you hear footsteps. The man is coming to investigate. Then the footsteps speed up. He must have seen Jane further along.

You hear a yelp from Jane as she takes off, and then a yell from the man chasing her.

As soon as the man passes your position, you rip off your camouflage and race down the path after him.

A shout of alarm followed by a loud thump tells you the trap has worked. Around the next bend, you find the poacher lying on the path cursing and struggling in the net. The more he struggles, the more the nylon snags his feet and arms.

You grab a couple of loops from the pile you prepared earlier and slip the sturdy vines over his shoulders pulling them tight around his torso and tying knots to hold them in place.

Moments later Jane arrives back on the scene. She leaps into the air and body slams the man on the ground like she's a big time wrestler.

"Oomph!" the man grunts as the air is forced from his lungs.

Jane jumps up and grabs some more vines and between the two of you the man is trussed up tight within minutes.

You pick up the walkie-talkie, and look down at him. "Well, well, what have we here?"

"You'd better let me—"

Jane kicks the man in the stomach. "You'd better hope my brother is okay mister!"

This is a side of Jane you didn't expect. It's like she's taken the whole ninja thing to heart.

"Stop it girly, or you'll be sorry."

Without hesitation, Jane kicks him even harder.

"Oomph!" the man grunts.

Jane glares down at him. "And don't call me girly old man!"

As Jane and the man lock eyes, you hear the crackle of the walkie-talkie.

"Jimmy, are you there?" More static, then a click. "Come in, Jimmy. Can you hear me?"

You look at Jane and grin. "Let the negotiations begin."

"If you don't want another kick, you'd better stop staring at me!" Jane growls at the man.

You make a mental note never to piss Jane off as you push the 'talk' button on the side of the transmitter. "Yeah Jimmy can hear you."

"Who's that?"

"Never mind who this is," you say into the microphone. "We have Jimmy and we want our friend back."

"You kids have Jimmy? Don't make me laugh. Come on, tell me. How'd you steal his transmitter?"

"We took it off him when we captured him. Now listen, we want you to let Adam go or we're turning your friend into the authorities. Kidnapping is a serious offence."

"If you've got Jimmy, let me speak to him."

"He's a bit tied up at the moment," you say. "Do you want to deal or do I go to the cops?"

There is silence for a minute. You suspect the two men are deciding what to do.

"We'll do nothing until you let us speak to Jimmy."

You hold the microphone near Jimmy's mouth and nod to Jane.

Jane gives him another solid kick.

"Oomph! Oh for Christ's sake, the brats have got me, alright! Do what they say and get me out of here while I still have some unbroken ribs."

You pull the transmitter away from Jimmy and speak clearly into it. "Here's what you're going to do. Bring Adam to the waterfall in exactly half an hour. That's where we'll do the exchange. If you don't show up, or if you show up early, we go to the authorities. Got it?"

Once again there is a brief silence before the man on the other end of the walkie-talkie comes back on. "Right. Half an hour."

"And Adam better be unhurt or the deals off!" you snarl before clicking off.

"Why the waterfall?" Jane asks.

You motion her out of Jimmy's earshot. "I have a

cunning plan."

"How cunning?" Jane asks.

"Cunning as a fox." Then you explain.

As you talk, Jane's grin gets broader. "You are evil ... but I like it."

"It should work, but we'll need to get moving to get in place before the men arrive. First we'll need to get Jimmy to his feet and make it so he can walk."

Jimmy isn't a lightweight. By the time you roll him onto his back, cut some net away so he has limited movement and maneuver him to his feet, you and Jane are both sweating in the sticky jungle heat.

You give Jimmy a little shove along the path. "Right Mister Poacher, get waddling."

Watching him walk is funny. Netting encases him from head to calf and his arms are bound tightly to his sides. He reminds you of a woman in a tight skirt as he takes small, awkward steps.

Whenever he slows down you prod him with a stick.

"Stop poking me brat, I'm going as fast as I can!"

The steep path leading up towards the waterfall doesn't help Jimmy's speed.

You wink at Jane. "Just keep it moving Mister."

When the three of you arrive at the waterfall you stop, splash some cold water on your face and then pull out your map. You show Jane the path you spotted on it earlier.

"See just here." Your finger traces a line that runs from

where you are standing, up and around the falls to the top of the cascade. "This is the path I was talking about. And here," you say, pointing to another line that leads from the top of the falls, around the far side of the volcano and back to the resort, "is our escape route."

"Perfect," Jane says.

You glance over at your captive. "Okay Jimmy time to do a little climbing."

Grabbing one of the vines tied around Jimmy's waist you lead him around the pond and up a narrow path. The track rises steeply. A couple of times Jimmy stumbles and you have to help him back to his feet.

After ten minutes or so the ground levels out and the trees and dense bush give way to flat slabs of rock. A rushing stream flows out of the jungle and thunders over the rocky ledge into the pond below.

Holding the vine around Jimmy's waist, you lead him to the edge of the rocky slab. Water rushes past beside you. When you peer over the edge, it is a straight drop to the water below, and because of the pool's clarity, you can see all the way to its bottom. "Whoa. That looks further than I expected."

Stepping back from the edge, you maneuver Jimmy so that he is visible from the path below and then stand slightly behind him holding tightly onto the vine so he doesn't trip and fall.

"Jane," you whisper, "can you go find our escape route?"

Jane nods then heads off while you keep an eye out for the poachers.

A few minutes later Jane's back, she cups her hand to your ear. "Found it. The path looks in pretty good shape."

"Excellent."

"What now?" Jane asks.

"Now we get Adam back."

"My friends are going to make you brats pay," Jimmy snarls from his perch.

"You know, for a man standing on the edge of a waterfall with his hands tied behind his back you're not very bright are you?" You nudge Jimmy a little closer to the edge with the stick. "You sure you want to piss me off right now?"

Jimmy peers over the edge and swallows. "Sorry kid. Don't do anything crazy now."

"That's better," you say, pulling him back a bit. Now keep your trap shut."

It's Jane's keen sense of hearing that alerts you to the sound of approaching footsteps.

"That's far enough!" you yell to the men when they reach the edge of the pool."

The men shield their eyes from the glaring sun as they look up at you. They have tied Adam's wrists but he looks okay.

"Untie Adam and we'll let your guy go," you say. "Adam, when they untie you, run up the path to the right of the falls as quickly as possible."

You see a tiny smile pass between the two men. You can tell they've got something planned … but then so do you.

"Okay, we're untying him now."

As soon as Adam's wrists are free, he does as instructed and sprints off up the path.

"Okay, and here's your guy. You'd better get him before he drowns." And with that, you shove Jimmy over the edge. "Bye bye jerk."

"Nooooooooooo!" Jimmy yells.

The splash sends a tower of water flying up.

"What the heck?" one of the men says as he dives into the water after Jimmy. The other man is about to run after Adam when his friend yells out. "Get in here. I can't hold him up on my own, moron!"

The second man dives into the water. When he surfaces the two of them are holding Jimmy's head above water and slowly dogpaddling back to a spot where they can get out of the water.

Jimmy is okay, but none too happy. "Just wait until I get my hands on those brats!" he splutters.

Moments later Adam arrives.

"Okay, time to get moving," you say.

"Hey thanks you two, good work," Adam says.

"Let's get out of here," Jane says. "We can congratulate ourselves once we're back at the resort."

Without any more mucking around the three of you scurry off into the jungle. You keep up a good pace but you're pretty sure your plan has worked and the poachers will try to leave the island quickly.

According to the map, the path you're on curves in a big arc around the slopes of the volcano. Being at a slightly higher altitude, this part of the mountain is covered in trees and broad-leafed shrubs, but every now and then you come across a patch of stunted growth trying to gain a foothold on top of an old lava flow.

At one such flow a pair of gray-brown birds with unusually large feet and orange legs are digging a burrow in the warm volcanic soil.

"Look, megapodes!" you say.

"Kwway-kwe-kerrr," the male bird sings.

"Kirrrr," the female replies.

"Funny looking things," Jane says. "What happened to the feathers on their throats?"

Below the bird's orange beaks is a sparse patch where the feathers look like they've been plucked.

"I think that's natural. I read these birds bury their eggs and then let the heat in the soil do the incubation."

"What? They just lay them and leave them?" Jane asks.

You nod. "I think so."

"Doesn't podes mean feet?" Adam asks.

"Yes," you say. "And mega mean really big."

"So we've discovered Big Foot?" Jane says, making a face of exaggerated astonishment.

Adam raises his eyes to the sky and sighs. "A big-footed

chicken maybe."

You laugh at Adam's joke. "Hey you two, we've made good time. Let's take a minute and grab a bite and something to drink. It's important to keep hydrated in these hot climates."

You pull out your drink bottle and an energy bar and watch the birds as you eat, glancing occasionally back along the track in case the poachers appear.

When you've finished you re-shoulder your pack. "Okay break's over, we'd better get moving." You start along the track again. "I hate to think what Jimmy will do to us given the opportunity, especially after his belly flop off the cliff."

The twins don't need much convincing.

After crossing the old lava flow the three of you re-enter the forest and continue your loop around the mountain towards the resort. Small streams cut their way down the rocky slope and higher up the mountain, large birds soar as they pick up thermals near the volcano's summit.

You are just starting to cross a tricky part of the track, where heavy rain has washed some of it away, when you hear a low rumble from deep underground.

Just as Jane swings her head around looking for the source of the noise, the earth starts shaking and the rumbling gets louder.

"It's an eruption!" Adam yells. "The mountain's going to blow!"

And here you were thinking the volcano was safe. But

then as quickly as the noise started, the rumbling stops.

You wipe the sweat off your forehead. "Phew! False alarm."

"Or prelude," Adam says.

You are about to move off, when you hear a strange clacking sound … and it's getting louder. When you look up the slope in the direction of the noise you see rocks and boulders tumbling down the mountainside.

"Rock fall!" you shout. "Run for it!"

The three of you scramble over the wash-out and hit the track sprinting. Thankfully the track is reasonably clear and without too many tree roots to trip you up. When the rocks hit the bush line, you hear the cracking of branches in the jungle behind you. Then a tortured creaking as the trees struggle to hold back the weight of the larger rocks. Then, once again, there's an eerie silence.

"Oh boy, that was close," Jane says.

"Not wrong there," you say with hands on knees sucking in deep breaths of air.

"This island is a death trap," Adam says. "Poachers, volcanoes, boulders bouncing down the mountainside. What next?"

Having caught your breath you walk over and slap Adam on the back. "Don't worry," you say. "At least we haven't had a tsunami."

"Yet," Adam says, trying to smile. "You do know eruptions cause tsunamis, eh?"

"Oh stop being a worry wart," Jane says. "We're ninja spies on a great adventure. Nothing can harm us."

You like Jane's optimism, but you also know that it's foolish not to have a healthy respect for nature. "Let's just keep moving and watch out for potential hazards. Even ninja spies aren't boulder proof."

A few minutes later, when the ground starts shaking a second time, you suspect the volcano is only warming up. You grab the nearest tree and hang on. After a minute's vibration, the mountain once again goes silent.

"I think its practicing for the main show," Adam says. "Let's just hope it doesn't do a Krakatoa on us."

Jane's brow creases. "Krakatoa?"

"You know, the Indonesian volcano that blew up and wiped out over 30,000 people," Adam says. "That eruption caused a huge tsunami that wiped out whole towns."

Jane raises her eyebrows. "But were any ninjas hurt?"

Adam mutters under his breath and rolls his eyes skyward.

Jane makes a face at her brother. "I didn't think so!"

"Well I don't know much about volcanoes," you say, "except that I don't want to be on them when they go off." And with that said, you take off down the path again.

"I'm with you," Adam says falling in behind.

"Ninja spies, evacuate the mountain!" Jane says as she jogs past the two of you. "Last one to the resort is a monkey's bum."

"See what I have to put up with?" Adam says.

Adam may find his sister a pain at times, but he follows her lead and increases his pace.

It's only another half an hour before the track cuts through a forest of pandanus palms, with their narrow spiny leaves and their strange stilted roots that look like mini teepees holding the main trunk clear of the ground.

When you come to a junction you stop and pull out your map. Adam and Jane look over your shoulder.

You point to a spot where two tracks meet. "We're just here I reckon."

"This track along the beach looks longer," Jane says tracing her finger along the line that runs along the coast.

"Yes, it's longer to the resort that way, but it's further from the volcano," Adam says. "The further we are from the mountain, the better."

"But what if the poachers are following us?" Jane says. "They could take the shorter track around the volcano and cut us off before we get to the resort."

The twins look at you expecting a decision. Do you:

Take the beach track? **P87**

Or

Take the shorter jungle track? **P100**

You have decided to go back to the resort for help.

You can't see any other alternative other than going back to the resort to get help. What are two kids supposed to do against three criminals?

"They said they'd hurt Adam if we said anything," Jane says. "Do you think they're telling the truth?"

You look at Jane's worried expression. "They could be bluffing."

"But how do we know?" Jane asks. "And what if they're not?"

Adam's capture is certainly a dilemma. It will take time to get back to the resort, even if you jog the whole way. The men on the yacht could be long gone by the time you get help from the resort.

You sit down, lean back against a coconut palm and think.

"Maybe you're right, Jane. What if they're not bluffing? They could dump Adam out at sea and deny ever having seen him. It would be their word against our. Could we even identify them properly? Remember if they've got Adam, they've got Adam's camera too."

Jane, normally so self assured, is looking shaky. "But what — what can we do?"

"I'm not sure but I think we need to try. Let's sneak back and see what they're up to eh? We might think of something."

Jane nods and then clenches her jaw in an attempt to look determined, but you see through her act. She's scared, and with good reason. Her brother is in danger and you may not be able to help him.

You step off the path and lead Jane into the jungle. "Hunters usually set their traps on paths."

"So that's why you're going off trail?" Jane asks.

"Yep. I'll lead us back to the cove cross-country, it may be harder going but we're less likely to run into trouble that way. You never know what booby traps the poachers have set up."

As the two of you work your way through the dense undergrowth, you hear the chatter of birds above you. You wonder if the birds are calling out a warning because you're in their territory, or just going about their normal business.

You figure you're about half way back to the cove when you see a thick length of black rubber stretching between two trees off to your left. The rubber is about eight inches wide and ten feet long. Interested, you veer towards it.

As you get closer you see fine mesh hanging below the rubber. "It's a net."

The rubber is suspended just above head level with the net hanging to the ground below.

"Why rubber?" Jane asks. "How does that help them catch birds?"

You have a look at the set up. "I don't think it is for catching bird."

Jane goes pale "Wha—what do you mean? Is it for ca—catching people?"

"Wild pigs more likely," you say with a grin. "The rubber will give some flex and stop the net ripping when one runs into it. See over there." You point to a pile of husked coconuts, their fibrous outer covering removed, leaving only the brown hard nut."Whoever set this up has been collecting coconuts too. More likely locals than poachers."

"They sure got a lot of them," Jane says.

Then an idea hits you. "Of course! Coconuts!"

Jane gives you a funny look. "Huh?"

"What's the same size as a coconut and used to be fired by pirate ships?"

"What? Pirate ships?"

"Cannon balls!" you say. "Coconuts are like cannon balls!"

"But we don't have a cannon," Jane says.

"But we do have the makings of a slingshot."

"We do?" Jane says.

You point to the thick band of rubber stretched between the two trees. "Yes. A big one."

A smile of understanding flashes across Jane's face as she sees where you're going. "So, your plan is to tie the rubber between two trees near the cove and fire coconuts at the yacht?"

You nod. "Exactly."

"But won't the poachers just pull up their anchor and sail

off?"

"They might if they can get to the bow of their boat without getting knocked out. Our job will be to stop that happening."

"You are evil," Jane says. "I like it."

"Right, let's get this thing down."

You climb up one tree and get to work untying the rubber. Jane climbs up the other. Once back on the ground you stand on one end and try pulling the strip of rubber up with your arms. The band is incredibly strong. With you knife you cut a coconut-sized section of net to use as your slingshot's pouch and attach it to the rubber. Then you take off your day-pack and fill it with as many coconuts as it will carry. Jane does the same.

You shoulder your pack. "Right, bombardier, to the beach!"

Jane winks. "Aar me hearty. Let's sink these buccaneers."

The two of you make a cautious approach to the beach in case the poachers have posted a lookout.

"Look for two trees about six feet apart," you say as you scout around.

Jane spots a couple up ahead. "How about these two?"

You inspect the trees, and then walk in a straight line back from the beach to check the firing line. The angle seems good. And there's a bonus. The trees she's pointed out have a row of low shrubs between them and the water. These shrubs will give you cover while you set up and, with a bit of luck, hide your position for a time while the poachers figure out where the flying coconuts are coming from.

"Perfect," you say. "Let's get set up."

Setting up the slingshot is a simple matter. You take a double loop around each tree at about shoulder height and tie a knot. Then you clear a path so you can stretch the rubber back as far as possible before shooting.

"These guys are going to freak!" Jane says with a grin.

After a final check that all is right you look over at Jane. "Ready for action bombardier?"

"Aye aye Captain."

"Load coconut," you say as you slip the first coconut into the pouch.

"St—retch," Jane says as the two of you grab the pouch and pull back as hard as you can.

"Elevation," you say kneeling down and angling your shot upward so it will have some distance to it.

"Three, two, one, FIRE!" you yell in unison.

With a *twang!* the coconut flies in a parabolic arc towards the yacht.

"It's a hit!" Jane exclaims as the rock-hard nut crashes into the side of the boat, leaving a small dent in the fiberglass.

"Load!" you yell.

The two of you quickly repeat the process.

"FIRE!"

The next impact has the men scrambling up from below.

"Can you see Adam?" Jane says.

One of the men is standing on the cabin top, looking your way.

"Quickly, let's get him!"

"FIRE!"

The coconut lands in the cockpit only feet away.

"Someone's shooting at us," the man calls to his companion. "Let's get out of here."

A man comes up from below and moves towards the bow."

"Let's get him!" Jane calls.

"Load!"

"FIRE!"

The coconut hits the deck a few feet from where the man is fiddling with the anchor rope. The shot's a miss, but it's close enough to give the man a fright and he scurries back to the relative safety of the cockpit.

"FIRE!"

This nut crashes through one of the yacht's side windows. There's more shouting from below.

Another man comes on deck with a pair of binoculars and scans the shore. The way he is sweeping back and forth means he hasn't spotted your position.

"Load," you whisper.

The two of you stretch back the slingshot. You take half a step to the right and aim at the man with the binoculars.

"Down a bit more," you say.

"Fire!"

The coconut screams out of the jungle. It is nearly upon him before he drops the binoculars and reacts. Unfortunately for him, he's too slow. The coconut doubles him over as it smacks into his pot belly. Then he staggers back and falls over the railing and splashes into the sea.

"Got him!" you say.

Jane points. "There's Adam."

The distraction you've created has allowed Adam time to open the front hatch and climb onto the bow. His hands are tied, but he steps over the railing and jumps into the water anyway.

"Give me your knife. I'm going to help," Jane says.

You reach in your pocket and hand it over.

"Cover me." And with that Jane streaks out of the jungle, runs down the beach and plunges into the water.

You load another coconut and pull back. Without Jane's help you really have to dig deep to pull the rubber back far enough, and you can't hold it long, or do much aiming before having to let go. But still you manage to fire three more nuts off in quick succession.

Thankfully, the men are too busy dodging coconuts and helping their friend get back on board to notice that Adam has jumped ship.

Adam floats on his back, slowly kicking his way to shore. As you fire another nut, you see Jane has nearly reached him.

She cuts the rope binding Adam's wrists.

Another nut hits the cabin top just as the men pull their friend aboard.

One of the men yells out. "The boy!"

"Fire!" you yell sending another nut flying through the air.

This one shatters a tray of food and drinks sitting in the cockpit. Glass goes flying.

"Let's get out of here," The injured man says as he drips on deck. "Get that anchor up!"

Jane and Adam are running up the beach. Soon you'll have a full crew of gunners again.

"Load!" Jane says as she grabs another coconut. "Let's teach these guys a lesson!"

With three of you the firing is much faster. Nuts zip though the air every fifteen seconds or so. Adam scouts around for more nuts, but after another five minutes you've exhausted your ammo.

"We'd better get out of here before they come ashore," you say.

"They'd better put the fire out before their boat burns you mean," Adam says.

You look at Adam. "What did you say?"

"Before I escaped I found a lighter and set the bunk in the front cabin on fire. It's polyurethane foam so it should burn like crazy."

"Holy moly!" Jane says with a grin. "My brother the arsonist."

Now that Adam's mentioned it, you can see a few wisps of smoke coming from the front hatch. The men have seen it too. One of them grabs a fire extinguisher from the cockpit and disappears below.

"Let's get out of here," Jane says. "I've had enough adventure for one day."

You look at the twins and smile. "There's always tomorrow me hearties."

Congratulations, this part of your story is over. You've saved Adam, and put a serious dent in the poachers operation. Maybe in another path you'll find some treasure.

It is time to make a decision. Do you:

Go back to the beginning of the story and try another path? **P1**

Or

Go to the list of choices and start reading from another part of the story? **P138**

You have decided to take the longer beach track.

"I think the volcano's going to blow," you say. "We'd better stick to the coast."

The twins follow as you veer left and head down the slope towards the sparkling water of the Pacific Ocean rather than carry on around the higher loop track.

Ten minutes later, when you feel another rumble beneath your feet, you're sure you've made the right decision.

Higher up the mountain, you hear rocks tumbling downhill and crashing into trees.

"I wouldn't want to be up there," Adam says, picking up the pace. "This mountain is angry about something."

As if to confirm Adam's point, a blast of ash and rock shoots out of the crater, peppering the upper slopes with rocks. The resulting tremor nearly knocks you off your feet.

"Crikey!" Jane cries out, in a poor imitation of an Australian accent. "Ground's jumping round like a kangaroo being chased by a pack of dingoes."

This time both you and Adam roll your eyes. But Jane's not wrong about the volcano. The mountain's definitely working up a head of steam.

The three of you keep up the pace, eager to get as far away from the eruption as possible and it isn't long before the track begins to level out. More ferns begin to appear and you can see the tops of the coconut palms in the distance. The ground under your feet is less rocky and the sound of waves breaking creates a gentle background to the chirping of the birds.

You're only half a mile from the coast, when you hear an explosion of some magnitude behind you.

"Holy moly," Jane exclaims. "The mountain's bleeding."

You look up through a gap in the trees. Near the top of the cone, blood-red lava flows out from vents in the volcano's flanks. Rivers of red run down the mountain, consuming everything in their path. Dense smoke billows into the air and with each explosion more rocks and debris are ejected high into the air.

A flock of lorikeets skim the treetops as they flee the upper slopes and you hear a loud crashing through the undergrowth that you suspect is a wild pig frightened by the rumbling.

"I wonder what's happening on the other side of the island," Adam says. "Do you think the lava will threaten the resort?"

You scratch your head. "It's possible. We'll find out soon enough I suppose."

When you come out of the bush onto the coast and look in the direction of the resort you see a curtain of smoke rising in front of you.

Jane grabs your arm. "What's that?"

"I hope I'm wrong, but I think one of the lava flows has made it all the way to the sea."

Jane frowns. "You mean we're cut off?"

You wave the twins forward. "I'm not sure. Let's check it out."

It takes about ten minutes to reach the lava flow. Its acidic smoke makes you cough. Thankfully a sea breeze is blowing most of the smoke is up the slope.

Only the lushness of the green tropical plants stops the fire spreading wildly across the island. Were it the dry season, heaven knows what sort of fires the lava flow would have started.

"It's wiped out the track," Adam says.

He's right. Although the lava is beginning to crust over, cracks show the fiery red, still fluid, lava running beneath.

You shake your head. "No way across that. We'd end up looking like overcooked marshmallows."

Adam looks nervous. "What now?" he asks.

"Goodness ... gracious ... great balls of fire," Jane sings in her best rock and roll voice.

Eyes roll.

While Jane tries to make light of your situation, you think hard about how to get out of this predicament. But then Jane surprises you with a suggestion.

"I've seen documentaries on TV. When lava flows into the ocean it makes lots of steam, but the water always wins in the end and cools the lava down. Couldn't we just swim around it?"

"I'm not that great a swimmer remember," Adam says.

But what Jane has said makes perfect sense.

"Let's go to the beach and check it out," you say. "We can always put some coconuts in our day packs for buoyancy."

"Okay," Adam says. "Anything's better than being captured."

"Or toasted," Jane says.

Where the lava meets the sea is a battleground. Hot lava flows forward and waves crashing on the shore put up a defense. Steam is everywhere. The lava crackles and pops as it is doused with cold seawater, but still it keeps coming.

"How wide is the flow do you think?" you ask the twins.

"Two hundred yards maybe," Adam replies.

"Easy-peasy," Jane says. "We can swim that no problem."

You put your pack on the ground and look around. "Okay let's gather some coconuts. And make it quick, this mountain isn't getting any friendlier."

If there is one thing this island isn't short of, it's coconuts. Within a couple minutes your packs are full to bursting.

"These are heavy. You sure they'll float?" Adam asks.

You raise your eyebrows at Adam. "Coconuts float all over the Pacific silly. Is your pack lighter than it would be if it was filled with water?"

Adam lifts his pack by its straps. "Yeah, I suppose…"

"Well anything lighter than water will float. There's lots of air trapped by the coconut's husk. Believe me, they'll float just fine.' You lift your pack and sling it over your shoulder.

"Come on let's go."

There is no protective lagoon on this part of the coast. You'll have to enter the water from the rocks. You find an area where an old lava flow protrudes into the sea and walk out onto it.

"Time your leap so you get sucked out by a retreating wave," you say. "And don't lose hold of your pack."

Adam looks nervous.

"I'll go first," Jane says. "I'm the strongest swimmer. Once I'm in the water, I can help if one of you gets has problems."

Again Jane is making a lot of sense. You nod and watch as she shifts her pack onto her chest and puts her arms through the straps.

"Look guys, I'm the hunch stomach of Notre Dame."

Your eyes roll, "Enough with the jokes already," you say, but secretly you're pleased that Jane has a sense of humor. It will make things easier for Adam when it's his turn to jump.

Jane moves further out onto the rock and gets ready to leap. As a wave breaks, the white foam rushes up around her ankles, then as the water surges back, she takes two quick steps, leaps in, and is sucked out with the retreating wave.

She paddles out beyond the next wave and then turns back toward shore. Her day pack holds her upper body well above the water. "See, I told you. Easy-peasy."

You and Adam repeat the exercise without any drama and start swimming out around the lava flow. You're pleased you took your face mask out of your pack and put it in a side pouch. The sight below is spectacular.

Lava, red and burning, like an undersea river, flows out along the sea bed. Tiny bubbles rise from the boiling water where the lava touches the ocean. You can feel the heat radiating from the lava flow and are careful not to stray too close.

Then suddenly there is a silver flash beneath you. Then another. Your heart races, thinking that sharks have surrounded you, but then a dolphin jumps out of the water and twirls in the air before splashing down.

"Dolphins!" Jane yells. "Hundreds of them."

"I wonder if they're attracted by the heat of the lava?" Adam says.

More and more dolphins join in the fun as they leap over you, around you, and swim under you.

"So cute!" Jane squeals as a young dolphin comes up to investigate these new creatures that have invaded her territory.

Then after a series of gravity defying leaps, each more spectacular than the previous, the pod swims west and the dolphins disappear.

"Wow that was amazing," Jane says.

The dolphins have taken your mind off things and before you know it you have reached a spot where it's safe to come ashore. The place you've chosen isn't so much a beach as it is a channel in the rock between two old lava flows. Seaweed clogs the sides of the channel, but there looks to be a clear run up the center into shore.

You put your face down in the water, and kick your feet. Fish are everywhere. Sea urchins and hermit crabs crowd the bottom. It's like looking into an aquarium.

One type of coral looks like miniature red trees that have lost their leaves. Another resembles a pale blue brain. Anemones wave their tentacles and seaweeds of yellow and green sway gently in the tide. Electric-blue fish swim lazily by, while schools of red, white and orange striped fish move as one in shoals of a hundred or so. A bright yellow fish the size of a dinner plate nibbles at something on a lump of pale white coral and orange sea stars move slowly across the rocky bottom looking for shellfish to eat.

You're only twenty yards from shore when you see something sparkle. You stop kicking and float in place. Then you see it again.

You lift your face out of the water. "Stop, I see something on the bottom." You pass your sodden daypack to Jane. "Can you hold this please? I'm going to take a closer look."

After a deep breath you kick for the bottom. Once there you hold onto a piece of kelp to keep from floating up. Now where was that...

And then you see them. A trail of gold coins running along the eastern side of the channel.

In need of air you shoot to the surface. "Coins on the bottom," you tell the others when your head breaks the surface. "Heaps of them!"

"Holy moly," Jane says with a big toothy grin. "We're gonna be rich."

Jane passes Adam the two packs and you and she dive again. This time you manage to pick up half a dozen coins before having to resurface. With each dive, you find a few more coins, but it becomes obvious fairly quickly that this isn't the mother lode.

"How many coins have we got altogether?" you ask Adam who has been looking after the coins as you and Jane do the diving.

Adam does a quick count. "Twenty seven. What's the price of gold?"

You try to remember what you saw online before you left for your vacation. "About 1200 U.S. an ounce I think."

It's time for some quick calculations. You decide to multiply 30 times 1200 and then subtract 3 times 1200 to make it easy.

"Let see, 3 times 12 is 36. Put the three 0's back on and that's 36,000. Less 3 times 1200 which is 3600. That means we've got 36,000 less 3600. Or 32,400 dollars worth."

"Crikey!" Jane says. "That'll buy a few kangaroo burgers."

The three of you are congratulating each other when you hear a male voice nearby.

"There those brats are!"

You look towards land, but see nothing. Then you hear the low rumble of a diesel engine.

"The poachers aren't chasing us by foot," Jane says. "They've come by boat."

"They must be trying to beat us back to the resort," Adam says.

"No time to wait," you say, retrieving your pack from Adam and kicking towards shore. "Let's get out of here before they launch their dinghy."

Scrambling up the rocky beach, the three of you dump your coconuts and rejoin the coastal path. The men motor just off shore, watching you as you go.

"How are we going to shake them?" Jane asks.

"That's a good question Sis," Adam says before turning to you. "How are we going to shake them?"

"Let's just keep going. What can they do once we're back at the resort?" you say.

Your eyes follow the yacht as you walk quickly along the path. The volcano is still spewing ash and lava, and every now and then you feel the ground shaking.

Then a violent jolt knocks you off your feet.

"Holy moly," Jane says picking herself up. "That was the strongest one yet."

"Too big for comfort," you say. "I'm not liking this."

As you start moving again, you notice the sea receding. Where once there was water, now you can see fish flopping about. "That's odd," you say.

"Not odd," Adam says. "It's a tsunami!"

You look out to sea. A wall of white water is heading

towards shore. "Run!"

The three of you drop your packs and move quickly away from the beach. "Keep running for high ground," Adam yells. "Who know how far it will come inland."

As you dodge trees and palms and head further inland the ground gradually rises. With the volcano still erupting you don't really want to climb too high, but then you don't want to get caught by the incoming wave either. Then you hit an old lava flow where the ground rises steeply. You take a narrow path up the side of the flow, pumping your legs for all they're worth.

By the time you get to the ridge, you figure you're far enough from the beach to be safe. You breathe hard and watch the wave approaching the yacht.

"They've seen it coming," Adam says. "They're trying to turn their bow into the wave."

The three of you watch, spellbound by the sight unfolding before you.

As the wave rushes in, the bow of the yacht rises, and rises. It looks as though it's going to make it over, but then the sheer force of the water forces the yacht back. When the bow drops, and the boat turns side on to the wave, you know the boat is doomed.

As the seabed shallows near the shore, the wave rises, and rises, and rises.

"Holy moly!" you say, stealing Jane's favorite expression. "Look at it go!"

The yacht is on its side, mast down in the water. You can see the men hanging on for dear life as the wave pushes the boat towards the land. The suddenly the yacht capsizes, the mast snaps and the men are tossed in the water.

"I don't like their chances," Adam says as the wave rushes to shore.

Soon after the yacht is smashed on the rocks, the wave retreats. This is a bad as its arrival. Everything and everyone is sucked back out to sea.

Once the wave has gone, the three of you walk down to the water, amazed at how the area has been stripped clean of vegetation, and anything else the wave could take with it. Much debris floats offshore.

"Our packs are gone," you say. "And the gold."

"And the poachers by the looks of it," Adam says. "Unless they managed to grab something to keep afloat."

You walk to the water's edge, searching for survivors. There is no sign of the men. Then as you're looking around, you see a glint of something in a tidal pool. You hop over a couple rocks and bend down to investigate.

It's a gold coin. Then you see another. "Hey look," you say, holding the coin up between your thumb and index finger. "Gold!"

"There's a couple over here too," Jane says, picking up a coin. Then she does a little dance and twirls. "There're all over the place!"

And she's right. The tsunami has picked up coins from

the seabed and thrown them up onto the shore. The gold, being so heavy, got trapped in the cracks in the rocks and was left behind when the wave retreated.

As the three of you spend the next ten minutes searching, you wonder if this is the *Port-au-Prince's* treasure that the wave has picked up on its rush to shore.

"We could spend the rest of the day hunting for coins," you say, "but we should probably get back to the resort and see how things are. People could be hurt. If things are okay, we can come back tomorrow. Besides," you say, pulling a handful of coins from your pocket. "We've got plenty already."

So that's what you do. Half an hour later, as you round a protective headland you see that the resort survived the tsunami and everyone is fine. Even the volcano has gone back to sleep.

After reporting what happened to the yacht and answering a few questions over the phone with the police back in the capital, the three of you sit on the beach with a cold soda and watch the reds and oranges of the tropical sunset.

"Looks like we're coin collecting tomorrow," you say to the twins.

Adam gives you the thumbs up. "Meet by the pool after breakfast?"

"Sounds like a plan," you say.

"Crikey," Jane says as the last of the sun dips below the

horizon. "We're gonna be rich!"

Congratulations you've reached the end of this part of the story. You've survived a volcanic eruption, tsunami and being chased by poachers. Well done!

Now it's time to make another decision. Do you:

Go back to the beginning of the story and try another path? **P1**

Or

Go to the list of choices and start reading from another part of the story? **P138**

You have decided to take the jungle track.

The mountain is quiet again so you decide to take the much shorter jungle track to the resort.

"I think speed is the critical factor here," you tell the twins. "The sooner we get back to the resort the better."

"I'm with you," Jane says.

As you proceed along the path, overhanging tree branches block out the sky and the jungle is eerily quiet.

"This place is spooky," Jane says, sticking close to you and Adam.

About a quarter of a mile along, you come to a fast-moving stream that has cut a deep chasm down the side of the mountain in its rush to get to the sea. From a rocky ledge at the chasm's lip, you look down. A narrow track zigs down, crosses the stream at the bottom, and then zags back up and out the other side.

"Watch your step, these rocks might be loose," you warn the twins as you carefully take your first step down the steep bank.

When you reach the bottom you wait for the others. Adam is first to arrive.

"That rock looks slippery," he says, pointing down at the smooth basalt on the bottom of the stream bed. "Maybe we should lock arms as we cross so we don't fall over."

The stream is only calf deep, but the water is rushing past at quite a pace. Below, in the darkness of the chasm you hear the sound of tumbling water, a waterfall perhaps, so keeping your footing is important.

The three of you link arms and take small tentative steps as you start across.

"You're right about the rock being slick," Jane says, tightening her grip on your arm.

The crossing is only ten or twelve steps, and you're nearly there when you and the twins are knocked off your feet by another big quake.

With a splash, you find yourself sitting in water up to your waist and sliding down the smooth rock deeper into the chasm.

"Hang on!" you yell. "Keep your feet below you for protection!"

The three of you, with arms still linked, are pushed at an ever increasing speed down the natural waterslide worn into the rock. There is nothing to grab onto and no place to get out. All you can do is go with the flow.

"Yikes!"Jane screams as the three of you go flying over an eight foot waterfall.

Thankfully the pool is deep enough so you don't hit bottom when you splash down, but you've barely had time to get over the shock of the drop and catch your breath before the power of the water whisks you downstream into the next half-pipe.

"Keep your arms linked," you tell the others, knowing you've got a better chance of survival if you stick together.

The deeper you slide into the chasm, the darker it gets.

When the gradient suddenly steepens to almost vertical and you see a tunnel entrance coming up. There is nothing you can do.

"We're going underground!" you yell.

Instantly it's so dark you can't even see the twins.

Adam's been quiet so far, apart from the odd grunt as he's struggled to keep his head above water, but now that you've gone underground you can hear him whimpering. Or is that you?

If this slide had been at a fun park, you'd be having the time of your life, but not knowing what is coming up next in the total darkness makes this the scariest thing you've ever experienced.

The slide seems to go on forever. It twists and turns, dips and dives. At times you hear a drop coming up, and at others you just fall into space not knowing how far you'll fall before you hit whatever's at the bottom.

Even though you're sliding quickly, time seems to move very slowly. It's like your brain has switched to survival mode. Adrenaline surges through you.

After what seems like ages you feel Jane's arm tighten on yours.

"Is that light I see?" she says.

You suddenly realize you've had your eyes screwed tight. Sure enough there is a faint light coming from cracks in the rocky roof of the tunnel.

Then there's another drop of about six feet and you're deposited into an underground pool almost as large as the swimming pool at the resort.

Soft light filters down from above, giving the cave an ghostly feel.

"The water tastes salty," Jane says. "This pool must join up to the ocean."

What Jane says makes sense. Water always runs downhill towards the ocean. You must have slid through an old volcanic vent worn smooth by hundreds if not hundreds of thousands of years of water running through it to the sea.

The cracks in the rock above must be the result of tremors and erosion.

"Now we just need to find a way out," Adam says, not sounding all that confident.

"I've got my waterproof flashlight," you say, rummaging in your backpack. You breathe a sigh of relief when it still works.

The narrow beam shows a low roof of hardened lava.

"If the sea is getting in," Adam says, "there must be an opening somewhere. We just need to find it."

"I'm the best swimmer," Jane says. "Give me the flashlight and I'll see if I can find one."

With flashlight in hand, Jane takes a deep breath and dives. You and Adam follow her progress as the light moves along the bottom of the pool, sweeping back and forth as Jane searches. About twenty yards away she comes up for air and then dives again.

It isn't until her third dive that she pops up with news. "I've found a passage!"

"Can we get through?" you ask.

"Fish are swimming in and out so we should be able to as well."

You and Adam dogpaddle over to where Jane is treading water. After taking a deep breath you dive down to check out the passage Jane has found. It's about fifteen yards long with faint light at the end of it. It looks plenty big enough to swim through.

You've just surfaced, when you feel a surge of water come pouring into the cave through the passage. The roof of the cave gets closer as all the extra water comes streaming in. Then as the water rushes out again, it's about all you can do to keep from getting sucked out with it.

"Man that tidal surge is strong," you say. "If we're going to get out of here we'll have to time our exit carefully."

Adam, being the weakest swimmer, looks petrified.

Jane sees her brother's nervousness. "Adam and I can link arms and go together."

The look of relief on Adam's face is immediate. "Yeah, that way we'll have twice the kicking power."

You could mention that they'll also have twice the bulk to move through the water, but there is no point in undermining his confidence. "Okay," you say. "That's a good idea. Do you want the flashlight?"

"Nah," Jane says shaking her head. There's plenty of light coming from the other end. We'll be fine." Jane looks at her brother. "You ready?"

Adam swallows loudly and nods.

"Okay, here comes the next wave," Jane says. "As soon as it starts going out, dive and kick like crazy."

The siblings link arms and tread water waiting for the water to start its outward journey.

"Three, two, one go!" says Jane taking a deep breath and diving.

You watch nervously as the twins disappear into the underwater tunnel especially as it's your turn next. You put your flashing back in the side pocket of your daypack and get ready to dive. You have time for three deep breaths before you feel the water in the cave begin to rise.

As the water starts to surge out, you take one last breath and dive. At first the pull of the water is slight, but as you enter the passage, and the volume of water is restricted, the pull is stronger and you barely need to kick. Most of your efforts are around trying not to scrape along the rough sides of the tunnel. The last thing you want is to end up in the sea with cuts bleeding into the water. Sharks might think you're lunch.

You forget about sharks as you spot an old anchor leaning against one wall of the tunnel. You wonder briefly if it might be from a pirate ship, but then before you know it, you see sunlight streaming down from above and you kick hard for the light.

When your head breaks the surface you look for Jane and Adam.

"Pssst!"

You look around for the noise.

"Pssst! Over here."

You turn to your right and see Jane and Adam hiding behind a rock. Then you see the poacher's yacht bobbing gently in the cove between you and the beach.

You can't believe your eyes. You've been washed down the mountain all the way back to Smugglers Cove!

"Get over here before they see you," Adam whispers, signaling you over.

Thankfully the men on deck have their backs to you.

You dive down and swim underwater towards the rock where Adam and Jane are hiding.

"We've ended up back where we started," you whisper. "This is one crazy island."

"And those horrible poachers are still here," Adam says softly, careful not to let the men hear him.

You look around for a solution, but the rock you're hiding behind is about twenty yards from any other cover. If you try to swim to shore, the poachers could see you.

"We might have to hang here until nightfall," you say.

Then you hear a loud voice drift over the water from the yacht. It's Jimmy berating his friends.

"Why don't you lazy sods give me a hand with the last

couple of traps, then we can get out of here," he says. "I've had a hard day."

The two men laugh.

One of the men slaps Jimmy on the back. "Well at least if you decide to give up poaching, you can always take up cliff diving!"

"Shut up, you drongo!" Jimmy growls. "That fall almost killed me!"

The two men laugh again.

"Okay we'll help," the other man says once he's stopped laughing. "I don't want to be hanging around here when the authorities arrive."

The three men finish their drinks, climb down into the dinghy and start rowing away from you towards the shore.

You look at Adam and then at Jane. "Are you thinking what I'm thinking?"

Jane smiles. "A spot of piracy perhaps?"

"You got it."

"Those poachers will kill us," Adam says.

"Only if we get caught," Jane says. "And ninjas never get caught."

"It's worth the risk," you say. "If we hijack their boat, the only way they can get off the island is to come back to the resort. By then, we'll have the authorities waiting for them."

You look towards shore. The men are about half way to the beach.

"Once they've gone into the jungle we'll need to move

fast. Who knows how long they'll be gone," you say.

It isn't long before Jimmy and the other two men drag the dinghy above the tide and march off into the jungle with their cages. As soon as they've disappeared, you and the twins start swimming towards the yacht.

"Ever driven a boat before?" Jane asks as she dogpaddles beside you.

You shake your head.

"I've done a bit," Adam says. "My friend's father has a boat, how different can it be?"

"About thirty feet, I reckon," Jane says.

The ladder at the back of the yacht comes right down to water level so it's easy for you and the twins to climb aboard. When you reach the cockpit, you're pleased to see the key is in the ignition.

Adam has a look around and takes the role of captain. "We need to get the motor running and motor over the anchor to unhook it from the bottom. Then once we pull the anchor up, off we go."

Never having done much boating you take Adams word for it. "Jane and I can pull up the anchor."

Adam puts the gear lever on 'N' for neutral and turns the key. There is an immediate puff of black smoke from the back of the boat and a satisfying rumble of the diesel motor as it comes to life. Water from the exhaust pours from a hole in the stern.

"Right," Adam says. "I'm going to ease us forward over

the anchor so you two get hauling on that rope."

At first the rope refuses to budge, but then as the boat moves forward and the angle of the rope through the water changes, you feel movement.

"It's coming!" you yell back at Adam.

You and Jane coil the anchor rope on the deck as you pull. Just as the anchor comes out of the water you hear someone yelling from shore.

"Hey! What do you think you're doing?"

The men climb into the dinghy and one of them grabs the oars and frantically rows towards the yacht.

"Time to get out of Dodge, partner," Jane says in her best cowgirl accent. "Those pesky rustlers are back."

There is a surge of white water at the back of the boat as Adam pushes the throttle forward and the yacht picks up speed. For a brief moment Adam points the yacht out to sea but then he spins the wheel and brings the yacht back around.

"What are you doing?" you say. "Escape is the other way."

Adam pushes the throttle even further forward. The diesel engine is really racing now. The boat's speed increases.

You look at the indicator on the control panel. The yacht is doing nearly 11 knots.

You look at Adam. His face is wild. "I said, what are you doing?"

"Tidying up," Adam says, turning the wheel a bit to

starboard and pointing the bow of the yacht directly at the men in the dinghy.

"Holy moly!" Jane says. "You're going to ram them!"

The men are quick to realize what Adam is up to as well. The rower has turned the dinghy around and is now frantically trying to get back to shore. Unfortunately for the poachers, panic and good rowing technique don't usually go together. Within ten seconds the men realize the yacht is going to collide with the much smaller dinghy and leap into the water.

Adam, showing skills you never expected, steers the boat until it is nearly upon the dinghy and then pulls back the throttle a little and spins the wheel hard to the left, swerving the yacht at the last moment.

"Take the wheel and point her out to sea," Adams says to you as he grabs a boathook and leans over the side. With a sweep of the hook, Adam snags the abandoned dinghy's painter and pulls the rope aboard. Then with a couple of loops and a half hitch around a cleat on deck, the dingy is secured and the three of you are heading back out to sea with the dingy in tow.

"Good skills Captain Hook," you say to Adam. "That was one slick maneuver."

By the time you're out of the cove, the bedraggled men are arguing with each other back on the beach.

A few hundred yards off shore, Adam turns the yacht to the southeast.

"Right, to the lagoon," Adam says pushing the throttle slowly forward until the rev counter hits 2200 rpm. "Now we just have to find the gap in the reef and we're home sweet home."

"Gap in the reef?" Jane asks.

"Yeah, when we get close, one of you will have to climb up in the rigging so you can guide me through the passage into the lagoon. You can't see the coral from deck level. The light's all wrong."

Adam picks up the radio in the wheelhouse and flips on the power. "*Moneymaker* calling maritime radio, *Moneymaker* calling maritime radio, please come in maritime radio this is urgent."

The radio crackles. "This is maritime radio *Moneymaker*, what is the nature of your emergency?"

Adam explains the situation and then hangs up the hand piece. "Well that should do the trick."

"What do we do with all the birds below? Should we release them?" Jane asks.

"Better keep them for the time being. The authorities will need them for evidence," Adam says. "They'll let them go once they've taken photos I'm sure."

An hour and a half later, as the yacht rounds the headland and the first resort buildings appear, Adam points to the southwest. "Nearly there. One of you'd better get up the mast as far as the first set of spreaders."

"Spreaders?" Jane says.

"Those metal cross-members sticking out from the mast that are holding the rigging in place," Adam says.

"Oh, okay," Jane says crossing the deck and putting her foot in the first of the aluminum steps attached to the mast. "Arrr, this should be fun me hearties." And with that she scampers up the mast like she's been at sea all her life.

"I'll cruise along the reef, you tell me when you see a gap big enough for the boat to fit though," Adam yells up to his sister.

Jane, throws one leg over the spreader like it's a horizontal bar in gym class, wraps her arm around the mast and concentrates on the reef. A few minutes later she calls out. "Gap ho!"

Jane points to a spot on the reef where the water is calmer.

"Okay," Adam says swinging the bow around towards the gap. "I see it. Yell out if I get off course."

"Aye aye, Captain Hook."

Within minutes the boat is inside the reef and you're dropping the anchor. Tourists watch from the beach. A float plane sits by the wooden jetty. You notice that two of the people on the beach are dressed in uniform.

When the anchor is on the bottom, Adam tells you to pay out a bit of extra rope and then tie off to the sturdy post near the boat's bow. Then he puts the motor in reverse and digs in the anchor before turning off the engine. "Welcome to paradise," he says with a smile. "The dinghy will be leaving for shore in exactly one minute."

"Aye aye," you and Jane say in unison.

"Hey," Jane says. "Before we go ashore, look what I found below." Jane shows you a small canvas bag filled with American dollars.

"Wow," you say with eyes agog. "Where did you find that?"

"In the main cabin, under some socks."

"So what do we do with it?" Adam asks. "Turn it in?"

You look at Adam and smile. "Why don't we discuss that as we row ashore?"

Congratulations, this part of your story is over. You've made it safely back to the lagoon, survived an eruption and foiled the plans of the lorikeet poachers. Well done!

Now it is time for another decision. Do you:

Go to the beginning of the book and try another path? **P1**
Or
Go to the list of choices and start reading from another part of the story? **P138**

You have decided to try to sink the poacher's boat.

Adam seems determined to sink the poacher's boat with or without your help. On his own he's bound to let emotion get the better of him and end up in trouble. You decide that it's better if you and Jane help. With three of you, at least there is a chance of success.

"Okay I'll help," you say. "But only if we make a plan and stick to it. No crazy stuff okay?"

"Glug, glug, glug," Jane says with a glint in her eye.

Adam gives his sister a smile then turns back to you. "What plan did you have in mind?"

Your left hand strokes your chin as you think. "Let's check in with our families and then meet up at the beach. We can plan our attack while we keep a lookout for the yacht."

The twins agree and head off towards their bungalow. As you walk through the compound you wonder what you've got yourself in to. Poachers are dangerous.

You think of all the things you'll need to do for the operation to be successful. You'll need to get onto their boat, release the birds, open a valve or drill some holes in the hull to let the water in and then get away unseen. And what happens if one or more of the men stay on board to guard the yacht?

After checking in with your family, you grab a couple more energy bars and head for the beach. Adam and Jane are already there when you arrive. Adam is fiddling with something under his beach towel.

"What have you got there?" you ask as you toss them each an energy bar.

Adam hefts the object. "When we were walking back to our room, I noticed one of the maintenance men working in one of the bungalows. His toolbox was on the verandah outside so I asked him if I could borrow a drill for a couple hours."

"To drill holes in coconuts," Jane adds, "for drinking the milk."

Adam lifts the corner of his towel and shows you a hand drill complete with a chunky half-inch wood bit. "A few holes with this bad boy should do the trick."

You run your finger over the edge of the drill bit. "Whoa that's sharp."

Adam gives you an evil looking grin. "I drilled a hole in a fence post outside our bungalow. Like hot steel through butter."

Jane giggles. She's enjoying the intrigue far more than she should be. "I can't wait to start."

"Let's not get ahead of ourselves," you say. "We have a few things to figure out first."

You sit in the sand next to the twins and start discussing possibilities. Nearly an hour has gone by when you see the yacht come around the headland in the distance.

"Here they come," you say. "The wind direction is

coming off the beach so they'll need to drop their sail and turn on the motor before they can come into the lagoon."

As the yacht gets nearer they drop the mainsail.

"Why have they got a man up in the rigging?" you say.

"He'll be there to spot the gap in the reef and guide the boat through," Adam answers. "There will be too much reflection off the water to see the reef from deck level."

Ten minutes later the yacht is 100 yards off the beach and the men have dropped anchor. The yacht rocks gently in the light chop.

The men waste no time. One of them climbs down the stern ladder towards the dinghy floating at the end of its rope.

"Fingers crossed they all come ashore," you say.

Jane stands up. "I'll grab a surf board." Without waiting for comment, she runs over towards a collection of boards leaning against a tree for use by the resort's guests.

Unfortunately, only two of the men climb into the dinghy. The last of them unties the dinghy's painter from the cleat on the deck and tosses it to the men in the small boat. Then he passes them a set of oars.

"Get some pictures as they come ashore," you say to Adam. "We need all the evidence we can get."

Jane lays the surfboard down in the sand and sits back down. "You never know. It might come in handy eh?"

"So what now," Adam asks. "How are we going to do anything when they've still got a guy onboard?"

You shrug and go back to thinking.

A few minutes later it's Jane that speaks up. "What if I pretend to be drowning? Do you think he'd leave the boat to save me?"

Her idea is a good one and it makes you think. What sort of men are the poachers? Surely he wouldn't let a young girl drown. Even criminals protect their kids.

Adam looks doubtful. "But will that give us enough time?"

"It might if Jane gets him to bring her in to shore and not back to the yacht," you say.

Then you explain the rest of your plan.

"You are evil," Jane says . "I like it."

Adam still looks unsure. "Jane would have to be pretty convincing."

"Do ya'll doubt my acting ability?" Jane drawls in a mock Southern accent, her hands clenched to her chest, eyelids fluttering. "I'll have ya'll know I'm a fine actor."

"Swoon all you like Sis, we're talking about criminals here. Who knows what they'll do."

Trying not to laugh at Jane's performance, you give a brief nod towards Adam. "Your brother's right, Jane, we need a plan B in case plan A goes wrong. Think you guys. What do we do if the guy stays on the boat?"

By now, the two men from the yacht are dragging the dinghy up onto the sand. The one in charge tells the other to stay by the boat and marches up the sand towards the resort.

Adam watches as the man passes the surfboards and disappears into the resort. "He may not be gone very long. I don't think we have time for a plan B."

Having seen the man's urgency as he walked past, Adam may well be right. "Okay. Adam, grab the drill and let's go. Jane, give us a few minutes to get in to position before you hit the water."

"Ya'll come back now," Jane says, fluttering her eyelids once more.

You pick up the surf board and carry it to the water. It's one of those old long boards so both you and he have no problem fitting on it.

Paddling in a wide arc, you come at the yacht from the seaward side. The man on deck has his back to you as he watches the activity on the beach. Then you see Jane swimming towards the yacht, her strokes strong and steady.

About twenty yards short of the boat, she starts splashing and yelling. The man on the yacht stands up.

"Help!" Jane cries out. "My legs have got cramp."

To add effect, Jane sinks below the water briefly before clawing her way back to the surface and repeating her plea.

The man on deck is torn. You can almost see his mind working as he decides what to do. Your entire plan depends on the next few moments. He paces up and down the deck of the yacht. No doubt he's been told to stay on board by the boss man. But he's unsure.

When Jane goes under for a second time, the man takes

off his shirt and shoes.

"He's going to save her," you whisper to Adam. "Come on mister dive in."

For a third time, Jane splutters and sinks below the waves and finally, the man steps over the railing and dives into the water.

When the man reaches Jane he flips her onto her back and starts side-stroking back to the boat.

Jane, realizing where he's taking her, starts to struggle."No, take me to my Dad."

For a moment the poacher hesitates, but then stops. Maybe he's just remembered he's got birds onboard.

Again Jane cries out to be taken to the beach. She becomes a dead weight, slides out of his grasp and sinks below the water.

The man gives up and does what she asks. Jane floats, allowing herself to be escorted to the beach. The 80 or so yards should take them a few minutes. You just hope it's enough.

"Go," you say.

You and Adam paddle flat out towards the yacht. When you reach the stern, you take the surfboard's leg strap and loop it around a rung of the ladder to keep it from floating away and scamper aboard.

The companionway hatch is open. Down four steps and you're in the saloon. On the floor sits two cages, each holding a twenty or so lorikeets.

"Let's get these cages on deck," you say.

The wire cages are awkward. The birds start making a racket when they see you.

Carrying an end each, you and Adam maneuver the cages up onto the deck. The birds are loud but thankfully the wind is blowing out to sea so most of the sound is carried away from the beach.

You take a quick look shoreward. Jane and the man are only thirty yards from the beach. "I'll let the birds out, you get drilling."

Adam heads below while you open the cages. The lorikeets waste no time in flying off.

After throwing the cages overboard, you stick you head through the companionway and look for Adam. You hear sounds coming from one of the cabins. "Drill quickly, because as soon as Jane hits the beach we're out of here."

Keeping low behind the cabin tops, you watch Jane's progress. As she and the man near the beach she starts struggling again. You can hear her cries of panic as she twists in the man's grasp. Finally, when the man can touch bottom, he picks Jane up, throws her over his shoulder and marches to where his companion is waiting beside the dinghy.

Jane pretends to be in distress, arm flapping, coughing and gasping for breath. Her rescuer moves Jane into the recovery position and hovers over her until one of the staff from the resort comes over to see what is going on.

"Okay time to go!" you yell down to Adam.

Adam appears from the depths of the boat. "The water's not coming in fast enough!"

"Well we can't stay here any longer!"

Then Adam sees something in the galley that attracts his attention. He grabs the bottle of mentholated spirits and starts pouring it all over the seat cushions.

"Hey," you yell, "this isn't part of the plan!"

"It's the new plan B," Adam says, striking a lighter he's found by the stove and setting fire to one of the seats in the saloon. "Let's hope these cushions are polypropylene. Burns like crazy that stuff."

Smoke begins to fill the cabin.

"Adam, we've got to go now!"

The two of you rush to the stern and leap into the water. You untie the leg rope, climb on the surfboard and start paddling like crazy, not towards the beach, but parallel to it away from the yacht.

"The poachers haven't seen the smoke yet," you say to Adam as you look over towards the beach. "Correction, they've just spotted it."

The two men are frantically dragging the dingy into the water. The larger of the two grabs the oars and starts rowing as fast as he can.

The men don't notice as you and Adam join another group of people mucking around on surfboards and wind surfers in the lagoon.

"I think we've done it," Adam says.

Adam was right about the polypropylene. Thick smoke billows from yacht. By the time the men in the dinghy row to the boat, the flames are too intense for them to get aboard. When a series of loud bangs start popping, you can only assume ammunition of some sort is going off inside the boat.

"It's a lost cause!" the man with the oars yells as he starts rowing back to shore.

By now there is a crowd on the beach. It includes the head poacher who is waving his arms and talking to a male staff member.

"See the guy on the beach with the poacher dude?" you say to Adam. "He must be their contact. We must get a picture of him when we get ashore."

"The boss man doesn't look too happy," Adam says.

You and Adam reach the beach at about the same time as the two men in the dinghy.

As you join the other tourists watching the burning boat, you edge closer to where the poachers are standing. The head poacher is cursing at his companions as if the fire were their fault.

Jane, now fully recovered, sees that the two of you are back on the beach and comes over to join you. "Good skills," she says. "Ninjas one, poachers nil."

Adam unzips a pocket in his shorts and pulls out three items about the size of small candy bars. "Wrong again, Sis.

Ninjas three, poachers nil." And with that he drops a gold bar into each of your hands. "One each … just don't let the poachers see them."

"Where did you get these?" you say, turning your back to the poachers.

Jane's eyes are bulging, but she wastes no time slotting her bar into the pocket of her shorts.

"When I opened a floor panel to drill a hole, they were just lying there. I didn't see any point in leaving them behind."

You have a closer look at the ingot and read the small writing stamped into it. "One Ounce 99.9 per cent pure."

"What's that worth, I wonder?" Jane says

"Last I heard gold was over twelve hundred US dollars an ounce," you say.

"Wow," Jane says. "Being a ninja pays pretty good."

Adam puts his bar back in his pocket. "I'm going to donate mine to the Animal Rescue people."

You think for a moment at what you'll do with your share, but then realize you've got pretty much everything you need. You're on vacation on a beautiful island. You've got friends. Hey what else do you need?

You pass your ingot back to Adam. "Here, give them mine too. I'll just blow it otherwise. It may as well do some good."

Jane shakes her head. "But, I need shoes and dresses and—and… Just joking," she says, handing her ingot back to Adam. "I wouldn't feel right spending ill-gotten gold on myself anyway."

Adam tucks the gold away. "Thanks you two. This will make a big difference."

You shrug. "It's only money."

As the three of you watch the last of the boat disappear, you notice the sun is dipping below the horizon. Reds, fiery oranges and every color in between contrast the sparkling blue of the lagoon. The rocky point, shaped like the dolphin's nose at the far end of the lagoon is just a silhouette.

"So what adventure are we having tomorrow?" Jane asks.

"We've still got treasure to find remember?" you say. "Meet you here on the beach after breakfast?"

"Arrr me hearty," Jane says in her best pirate accent.

"Arrr," Adam says joining in the fun.

"Arrr," you say, trying to keep a straight face.

The next thing you know, everyone is laughing as the three of you head back to your families, excited at what tomorrow may bring.

Congratulations you've finished this part of your story. You have successfully stopped the poachers and found some gold which will go to a good cause. Well done!

But have you tried all the tracks?

Are there other dangers on Dolphin Island?

It is time to make another decision. Do you:

Go back to the beginning of the story and follow another path? **P1**

Or

Go to the list of choices and start reading from another part of the story? **P138**

You have decided to contact the authorities.

"Let's not do anything radical," you say. "Better we find a way to contact the authorities without anyone from the resort finding out and let them deal with the poachers. Using the resort's phones is out because of the calls having to go through reception, that's going to limit our options."

The three of you are silent a moment, as you each try to come up with a solution.

"I've got it," Jane says. "Boats have radios, right?"

"Yes…" you say hesitantly wondering where Jane is going with this.

"And the police have radios?"

"Yeah sure."

"Well there must be at least three boats in the lagoon. Surely one of them has a radio we can use." Jane looks like she's just eaten the last chocolate in the box.

"But the poachers have a boat too Sis," Adam says, countering her argument. "And if they hear our transmission they'll scarper. Then your whole plan goes down the gurgler."

Jane frowns. "Hmm … I didn't think of that."

"But what if they didn't hear the transmission?" Adam says."What if their radio antennae were out of order?"

You give Adam a questioning look. "And how do you plan on achieving that?"

"Well," Adam says. "I've done a fair bit of fishing with

my friend and his dad. I can cast a lure pretty much wherever I want."

"Okay," you say. "But how's catching fish going to help?"

"Well," Adam continues, "if I cast a wire trace, with a big lure on it, over the yacht's antennae, and then start reeling in, I might be able to rip it off."

"You really think that will work?" you ask.

"I really think we should give it a go. What have we got to lose?"

"I'll admit, little bro's pretty good with a rod," Jane says. "Streuth, she's worth a crack!"

Two sets of eyes roll at the return of Jane's Aussie accent, but after some further discussion the three of you decide to try out Adam's plan.

"Right," Adam says. "Jane and I will rent one of the resort's small motor boats. Then we'll drop you off near one of the larger boats moored in the bay so you can get to their radio. Then, with Jane steering, I'll hook the antennae and then we'll motor off at top speed and do our best to rip the antennae off the poacher's mast."

"Sounds like something out of a movie," you say, wondering if the scheme will work.

"I'm not so sure. Fishing ninjas doesn't quite have the same ring to it." Jane says with a giggle.

After renting the strongest pole and tackle he can find. Adam rigs up a line. Then the three of you climb aboard the runabout you've rented.

"Which boat should we try?" Adam asks.

You look at your choices. "That marlin boat's pretty flash. It's bound to have reliable VHF."

Adam turns the key to start the runabout. "The marlin boat it is then."

Jane grabs your arm. "There they are, right on schedule!"

You and Adam turn your gaze towards the reef. Sure enough the poacher's boat is heading into the lagoon.

Your runabout starts first pop. Jane unties the bowline from the jetty and Adam pushes the throttle forward.

As he points the bow towards the reef Adam yells over the roar of the 25hp outboard. "We'll do a loop and approach the marlin boat from behind so nobody from shore sees what we're up to. You'll have to jump overboard and swim the last 10 yards or so."

You swallow, and try to steady your nerves. "Just what I always wanted to do while on vacation, jump from a speeding boat."

Jane laughs. "Think of it as walking the plank. At least it's better than being keel-hauled."

You're getting close to the marlin boat.

"Okay, get ready to jump," Adam says. "I'll slow down the boat, but only for a moment. Oh and don't forget to use channel 16, that's the emergency channel."

Thirty seconds later, Adam throttles down and you leap over the side. Immediately he's back on the gas and bouncing away over the slight chop in the lagoon.

Thankfully the marlin boat has a ladder on its stern. You make your way into the wheelhouse and look for the switch to power up the radio.

After turning on the radio you look at the screen and see the radio is already set on the right channel. There is a crackle of static and you hear brief conversations come over the speaker.

You lift the handset out of its cradle and get ready to transmit.

Meanwhile, Adam has swung the runabout in a lazy arc and is heading to where the yacht is busy dropping anchor. Jane takes the controls as Adam lines up his cast.

The poachers antennae is a slim rod sticking up from a bracket near the top of the mast next to a wind speed indicator, radar reflector, and navigation light. You can't believe he really thinks he has a chance of snagging such a small target.

Adam stands in the back of the runabout, his backside pressed against the transom for stability. The long pole is upright. As you watch, Adam practices his casting by flicking the pole back and forth trying to get a feel for it.

As the runabout nears the yacht, one of the men is busy securing the anchor, while another is preparing the dinghy to come ashore. Then two of the men climb down into the dinghy and start to head towards shore.

Jane turns the runabout and goes around for another pass.

By the time Jane lines up for the next pass, the men and their dinghy are halfway to the beach. Jane throttles back just as Adam whips the pole forwards, sending the lure flying high in the air.

The heavy lure passes clean over the bracket holding the antennae and Adam starts reeling for all he's worth. As Adam reels in, the lure stops midflight, drops and then hooks itself around the bracket. Adam fist pumps the air and then puts the pole into a special hole in the aluminum hull of the runabout designed to keep rods from falling overboard when fishing.

Jane lets out a rebel yell and steers the boat towards the yacht. When she's ten yards from colliding with the yacht she swings the runabout into a sharp turn and puts on more power.

As the runabout streaks away from the yacht the line tightens. At first the yacht's mast tilts towards the fleeing runabout and you're sure the line will break. But leverage is a wonderful thing and the line is stronger than you imagined. It holds as the yacht tilts further and further over.

The remaining man on deck trips and nearly falls over the side as the deck beneath his feet is suddenly no longer level. Then there is a wrenching sound as the bracket is ripped off the mast.

This time, as the deck tilts quickly back the opposite way, the man on deck is caught off balance again and goes flying over the rail.

You click the transmit button. "Maritime radio, maritime radio, maritime radio," you repeat three time as instructed by Adam. "Mayday. Come in maritime radio."

"This is maritime radio, what is the nature of your emergency?"

It takes you a few moments to explain the situation, but finally after a lot of back and forth, the operator agrees to call the police and pass on your message.

You thanks him, and look to see how Jane and Adam are getting on.

The man on the yacht is climbing up the ladder as Jane and Adam motor toward your boat.

You give them the thumbs up, switch off the radio and dive overboard. It's a short swim to the pickup spot. A minute later Adam helps you out of the water and onto the runabout. After wiping the salt water off your face you look over to the yacht.

"Did you get through?" Adam asks.

"Ninjas one, poachers nil," you say. "The police are on their way."

"Yippee!" Jane yells.

Adam smiles. "That's great."

Back at the yacht, the man is looking around, still wondering what hit him and how he got tipped into the drink on a perfectly flat lagoon.

"Let's hope he doesn't notice the missing aerial before the police arrive," you say to the twins. "What did you do with the antennae you caught?"

Adam points to the middle of the lagoon. "It's now a dive feature over there on the bottom somewhere."

It's a quick trip back to the resort.

After dropping off the runabout, returning the fishing gear, minus some trace and a lure, and grabbing some cold drinks, the three of you go and sit on the beach to wait for the police to show up.

As you wait, the two poachers and a man from the resort walk down the beach and climb into the dinghy.

"They'll be off to do the deal for the birds no doubt," Adam says.

You cross your fingers. "I just hope the cops show up soon."

Jane takes a long sip of her soda. "Looks like we'll have to find the treasure tomorrow."

"We've got all week," you say. "The treasure's been here for 150 years. I don't think it's going anywhere this afternoon."

"Unlike our poacher friends," Adam says, pointing to the gray patrol boat entering the lagoon. "It's going to be interesting to see how they explain all the birds on board."

Congratulations this part of your story is over. You've done well. But have you tried all the possible path the story takes?

Have you explored the waterfall and the volcano?

It is time to make another decision. Do you:

Go back to the beginning of the story and try another path? **P1**

Or

Go to the list of choices and start reading from another part of the story? **P138**

It's all about the math

"How did you do that so quickly in your head?" Jane asks. By now Adam is listening too.

"Well it's not exact," you say, trying to think of an easy way to explain it. "But the yacht can go in pretty much any direction right?"

The twins nod.

"A knot is 1.15 miles. So 8 knots is a fraction over 9 miles. That means there will be a circular search area with a radius of 9 miles, minus a little bit of land, right? Imagine a big circle with a dot in its centre. The dot is the yacht and the rest of the circle is a place the yacht could be, apart from the small bit of land that makes up the island of course."

Jane and Adam seem to be following your explanation so you continue.

"To calculate the area of a circle you square the radius, squaring means multiplying the radius by itself and then we multiply that answer by pi or 3.14.

"What a radius?" Jane asks.

"It's the distance from the dot in the middle of the circle to the outer edge of the circle. Like the spoke of a bike wheel."

"So the radius squared is 9 times 9 which is 81 and then we multiply 81 times 3.14?" Jane asks.

"That's right," you say. "I made it easier by working out what 3 times 81 was first. 3 times 80 is 240 and 3 times 1 is

3.

Jane's got the hang of it now. "So that's 240 plus 3 which equals 243."

You nod. "Then I take .14 and multiply that times 81. This is a bit trickier but when you realize .14 is the same as 14 per cent, it's easy. To get 10 percent of 81 you move the decimal point one place to the left or 8.1 ... let's call it 8 for simplicity. Then we take 4 percent of 81 which is a bit less than half of 10 percent ... so let's just estimate it and call it 3.

"So we have 243 plus 8 plus 3 which is 254," Jane says.

You smile. "That's right. Then we just need to take off a bit for the land area. Like I said it's not exact but it's near enough."

"It like working out a puzzle," Jane says. "Kind of fun when you think of it that way."

"Yep," you say. "And the more you learn the better the puzzles get. Math is full of sneaky tricks. It's just a matter of knowing them."

Without any further explanation, you turn and start down the path back towards the resort. You hear the twin's footsteps behind you. Jane mumbles numbers as you half walk, half jog through the jungle.

[Go back to the story **P46**]

Dolphin Island FAQs

Q. Is Dolphin Island a real place?

A. No, Dolphin Island is fictional island. However there are many islands in the South Pacific that have similarities to what has been described in this story. Polynesia means 'many island'. If you are interested in the area where this story is set, try looking up and reading about Tonga or Samoa.

Q. Was the *Port-au-Prince* a real ship?

A. Yes. The *Port-au-Prince* was a tall ship of 500 tons that carried 24 cannon. The ship was built in France before being captured by the British. It then became a privateer (legal pirate by license from the British government) and was sent to raid Spanish ships off the South American coast. After some raiding the *Port-au-Prince* sailed to the South Pacific to hunt whales for their oil. Sometime in 1806, while in the Ha'apai island group in the Kingdom of Tonga she was attacked by the locals and is presumed to have sunk somewhere nearby. It was never discovered how successful the ship had been in her raiding as all her treasure is presumed to have gone down with the ship. Many experts believe remnants of *Port-au-Prince* were found in 2012 off Foa Island in Tonga.

Q. Are megapodes real?

A. Yes. Megapodes are real birds that bury their eggs in the warm volcanic soil to act as an incubator. There are many interesting birds in the South Pacific region.

Q. What happened at Krakatoa?

A. Krakatoa is a volcanic island between Java and Sumatra in Indonesia. It exploded in 1883 killing somewhere between 36,000 and 120,000 people (depending on how the statistics were calculated). The bangs from the huge explosions (4 in total) were heard over 3000 miles away in Australia. Some say the main explosion could have been the loudest in history. The volcano ejected over 6 cubic miles of rock, ash and lava and the tsunamis and pyroclastic flows of hot ash and steam, destroyed over 150 villages. The area is still very active.

So what would you like to do now?
Go to the beginning and read another track? **P1**
Or
Go to the list of choices and start reading from another part of the book? **P138**

138

List of Choices

More You Say Which Way Adventures.

Lost In Lion Country

Between the Stars

Danger on Dolphin Island

In the Magician's House

Secrets of Glass Mountain

Volcano of Fire

Once Upon an Island

The Sorcerer's Maze - Adventure Quiz

The Sorcerer's Maze - Jungle Trek

YouSayWhichWay.com

Made in the USA
Middletown, DE
30 November 2015